I stopped breathing for several seconds. I'm sure Maddy did too.

For coming down the stairs was my dad and he was wearing . . .

I'm sorry, but I must stop for a moment.

The full horror of what I'm about to tell you has just hit me all over again. But I'm calmer now and ready to tell you everything.

Dad pranced down the stairs wearing that hideously yellow fun(!) shirt and a pair of tight, red leather trousers.

But it was what he was wearing on his head that caused my blood to freeze.

He was wearing a baseball cap with a gold logo and he was wearing it the wrong way round . . .

www.randomhousechildrens.co.uk

www.petejohnsonauthor.com

How many Pete Johnson books have you read?

MY PARENTS ARE OUT OF CONTROL

Pete Johnson

CORGI YEARLING BOOKS

MY PARENTS ARE OUT OF CONTROL
A CORGI YEARLING BOOK 978 0 440 87013 5

First published in Great Britain by Corgi Yearling,
an imprint of Random House Children's Publishers UK
A Random House Group Company

This edition published 2013

3 5 7 9 10 8 6 4

Text copyright © Pete Johnson, 2013
Cover and interior artwork © Nikalas Catlow

Set in Century Schoolbook 12.5/16pt by Falcon Oast Graphic Art Ltd

Corgi Yearling Books are published by Random House
Children's Publishers UK, 61–63 Uxbridge Road, London W5 5SA

www.randomhousechildrens.co.uk
www.totallyrandombooks.co.uk
www.randomhouse.co.uk

Addresses for companies within The Random House Group Limited can be
found at: www.randomhouse.co.uk/offices.htm

THE RANDOM HOUSE GROUP Limited Reg. No. 954009

A CIP catalogue record for this book is available from the British Library.

The Random House Group Limited supports The Forest Stewardship
Council® (FSC®), the leading international forest-certification organisation.
Our books carrying the FSC label are printed on FSC®-certified paper.
FSC is the only forest-certification scheme supported by the leading
environmental organisations, including Greenpeace. Our
paper procurement policy can be found at
www.randomhouse.co.uk/environment

MIX
Paper from
responsible sources
FSC
www.fsc.org   FSC® C016897

Printed and bound in Great Britain by Clays Ltd, St Ives plc

*This book is dedicated with grateful thanks
to my brilliant editor, Natalie Doherty*

*And to my nephew Harry Birch,
who listened to the story first*

AN IMPORTANT MESSAGE

This diary does not exaggerate.

At times it might sound kind of unbelievable. But it all really happened to me.

And it could happen to you too. In fact, it probably will.

But you needn't worry about that.

Not with me to help you. So I suggest you read my diary twice. The first time, just sit back and enjoy it, and if you'd care to laugh at any of my jokes, you'd make me really happy.

Then, the second time, sit forward and concentrate. You might even want to take some notes. Then afterwards you'll know exactly what to do the moment your parents—

But I'm jumping ahead. So I'll stop here and see you over the page.

Louis the Laugh

CHAPTER ONE

Mum and Dad Learn
Some New Words

Friday 20 September

6.00 p.m.

Mum and Dad have just peeped round my bedroom door. Once they'd have barged right in and sat down and watched me do my homework.

They never let me alone. Whenever I looked up, there they were. In fact, if I was in the loo for more than two minutes they'd call out, 'Are you all right?' and 'I hope you're doing something educational in there.'

Parent fatigue. That's what I suffered

from. Until they decided they were getting too pushy and reformed their ways. So now they just hiss at me from the doorway.

'So how's the revision going then, Louis?' asked Dad.

I couldn't tell them the truth. I like to protect them from the harsher realities of life. (But I'll tell you, dear diary – later.) So I just said vaguely, 'Oh, pretty good.'

'By the way,' said Dad, 'my new boss is coming round tonight for a meal.'

'This is a bit sudden,' I said. 'I bet he just invited himself.'

Dad gave a little smile. 'Something like that.'

'And I bet he looks as if he's been dead for three days,' I went on, 'just like your last boss did.'

'That's where you're wrong,' said Dad. 'He's quite young. And he just wants to get to know all his managers and their families infor-mally.' Dad gave another small smile. 'And tonight we're the lucky ones.'

'He'll be here about seven o'clock,' said Mum.

'The excitement is unbearable,' I said. Then

a terrible thought struck me. 'I'm not going to have to wear a suit, am I?'

'It'll only be for a couple of hours,' said Mum.

I groaned loudly. 'And I suppose when he arrives you want me to bow, curtsey and throw petals at him?'

'No, just be yourself,' said Dad.

'Really?' I grinned.

'Well, more or less,' added Dad hastily.

6.15 p.m.

My parents have gone now, so I can tell you what I've been keeping from them.

We had a big history test last week which everyone in my year at school had to take. Now written at the top of my paper in blood red is my result.

I got 4%.

Looking on the bright side, that's better than 3%. Not to mention 2%. And I could really look down on anyone who got 1%.

Only no one did. I got the lowest. Felt a right melon.

But I've only been at this school for two weeks so far and they're much further ahead in history than at my last one (at my old school we hadn't even reached the eighteenth century, while here they've hurtled through most of it already, if you're remotely interested, which I'm sure you aren't).

Anyway, they've said I can re-sit the exam next Tuesday. Only my parents think I'm sitting it for the first time next week.

Meanwhile, my school is expecting me to spend every second wading through all the mountains of notes they've given me to catch up. Just looking at them makes my head hurt.

Plus I've got a big problem. I have this very rare medical condition. I'm severely allergic to homework.

Just last week at home I recklessly pulled out a maths textbook. And straight away my face started to really tingle. The very next morning a giant red spot landed there. So to protect my skin, really, I've been avoiding homework ever since.

But here's the good news, the brilliant news, the . . . well, you get the idea. School is of no importance to me. In fact, I could leave now. Well, I have finally mastered the alphabet and can count to about four and that's all I need for my real life – making people laugh.

Even as I'm writing this diary I'm trying to think of something funny to tell you. My thoughts are full of jokes all the time. So there's really only one job I can do. And certainly only one job I want to do. Be a comedian.

And I won't rest until I've got my own TV show, at least. (I'd like it to go out on a Saturday night too, but I'm open to discussion on that one.)

Anyway, last summer, would you believe, my dream actually came floating towards me. I was almost on a TV show called *Tomorrow's Stars*. I just sailed through the first rounds. I made it all the way to the final round, but I wasn't picked to go on the TV recording. Everything had seemed like it was all coming together and then suddenly it was goodbye and get lost.

Still, my agent said the fact that I'd got so close to my dream proved I wasn't an amateur any more. No, I'm a semi-professional now.

Oh yeah, I've got an agent. What's more, I'm her only client. She's called Maddy and is the same age as me (she goes to a different school though).

We met at Drama Club. That's where Maddy told me she'd wanted to be a famous actress for as long as she could remember. She even landed a great part – Nancy in *Oliver!* But before she went on stage she threw up everywhere. And in the end her understudy had to play the part.

She knew then that her nerves would stop her going very far as an actress. So she's putting all her energy now into spotting talent.

And she's spotted me.

She believes incredible things will start happening for me very soon.

So do I.

I just wish they'd hurry up as . . . But now Mum's shrieking at me to get changed into my suit.

So I'll catch you again later.

9.30 p.m.
So there I was, with my glued-on smile and trussed up like a turkey in my suit. Elliot, my little brother, was suited up too. So was Dad, while Mum even had her very posh pearls on.

And then Dad's boss and his very pretty wife, Maria, slouched in. He was a scruffy-haired guy, in a beaten-up leather jacket, drainpipe jeans and dead cool trainers – completely the wrong clothes for tonight's meal.

Dad's boss must have been mega-embarrassed, but you'd never have guessed by the way he sauntered over to Elliot and me and said, 'Yo, lads, I'm Rup.' Then he touched fists with us. From any other adult that would have been beyond cringy, but somehow it wasn't with Rup – perhaps because he swaggered about our house like a visiting rock star.

Now Dad's got this hut down the garden which he's turned into a little office. So I expected him and Rup to disappear down there for a while to talk business. Instead, Rup just hung out with Elliot and me, saying to Dad, 'Young people are our future, so we've got to hook up with them. They're dead important people.'

And Rup fired all these questions at 'dead important' me. When he asked me what my favourite subjects at school were, I replied, 'Karate-chopping pencils and annoying teachers,' and Rup laughed so much he nearly fell off his chair. I liked him a lot after that.

'You're a funny guy,' he said, pointing at me approvingly. Then he pointed at Dad. 'And you've been with the company for over twenty years.'

'That's right,' said Dad, a little shyly. He'd taken his tie off and rolled up his shirt sleeves so Rup didn't feel so out of place, which was decent of Dad. 'I started right at the very bottom, of course.'

'And he keeps getting promoted,' I said, doing my bit to talk Dad up. 'That's why we had to move here.'

'It can't be easy for you,' said Mum, turning to Rup, 'being parachuted into a new company just a few months ago—'

'That's why I rely on people like your husband,' interrupted Rup. 'A man of such vast experience.'

'As long,' said Dad, 'as that's not a polite way of saying I'm old.' He and Rup had a good old laugh about that.

Then Rup said to Dad, 'Together we'll turn this company on its head. We've got a lot of people who've been plodding on in the same way for too long. Let's shake them all up.' He grinned at Dad. 'So, are you ready for the roller-coaster ride?'

Dad said he certainly was. I liked the way Rup made even work sound exciting.

And after Rup and Maria left for their 'crib' (as Rup put it), I said to Dad, 'Rup didn't seem at all bothered that he'd forgotten to wear a suit.'

'Why should he be bothered?' said Dad, with more than a trace of bitterness. I supposed Dad meant that because Rup was the boss he could wear whatever he wanted.

'Rup looked dead young, didn't he?' I said. 'How old is he?'

'Twenty-nine,' said Dad, and I'd never heard him speak so fast.

'I'd say Rup's the best boss you've ever had, isn't he?'

Dad just grunted and didn't seem nearly as happy as he had been when Rup was here. So to cheer him up I said, 'Hey, Dad, it's your birthday tomorrow.'

But he didn't look much cheered up by that news.

11

Saturday 21 September

4.30 p.m.

Dad's birthday. I got him a box of shortbread and a football, which when you kick it plays a tune. I know, I spoil him.

He was having a pretty good day up to about twenty minutes ago. That's when he remembered who'd soon be turning up for their tea: my grandparents – his parents.

My nan can speak four languages and never says anything cheerful in any of them. Grandad's a bit less gloomy, but not about modern life – he and Nan just don't like it. And if they could, they'd send it back and swap it for another era completely. They are never afraid to tell Elliot or me off either.

'If Nan tells me one more time to take my elbows off the table,' said Elliot, 'or asks me if I've washed my hands today, I'll tell her to mind her own business. I don't ask Nan if she's washed *her* hands.'

'You won't say a word,' said Mum firmly. 'You'll try and understand their point of view and . . . well, they don't visit very often.'

Then Dad announced, 'They've arrived,' with not a great deal of excitement.

7.25 p.m.

'So, Louis,' asked Nan, her perfume, which always reminds me of fly spray, landing on me like poison gas, 'have you settled into your new school yet?'

'Oh yeah, I'm settled all right,' I said vaguely, keen to change the subject.

But Nan wouldn't let it drop. 'And how are you getting on with your teachers?' she asked.

'I get on with them so well,' I said, 'I'm known as Teachers' Pet. They keep me in a cage at the back of the class.' Which I thought was pretty funny, but Nan just looked confused. 'You've been put in a cage . . .' she began. 'I don't understand what you're telling me.'

'It's a joke,' said Grandad, who looks like a bloodhound who's just heard some really terrible news.

'Well spotted, Grandad,' I said. 'Here's another one for you. What did the policeman say to his stomach? *You're under a vest.* Get it?'

Grandad actually gave a creaky, rusty laugh. He asked Elliot and me to come towards him. Then he handed us both crisp ten-pound notes. He's not stingy, I'll say that for him.

'Hey, Grandad, that's awesome,' cried Elliot.

Grandad immediately winced. 'You devalue the English language when you use words like awesome so indiscriminately. A magnificent view might be awesome or—'

Grandad can grumble on like this for centuries, so it was lucky Nan interrupted him by announcing, 'You won't believe what I found today.' I waited for her to produce some gold coins or a long-lost heirloom which would make us all zillionaires. Instead, she handed Dad a photograph.

When Dad saw it he jumped in his seat as if he'd just received an electric shock. Then he said softly, 'I've seen a ghost.'

'You've got a picture of a ghost?' asked Elliot eagerly.

'Well, in a way,' said Dad, still peering at the photograph. 'It's of me a long time ago. But wherever did you find it?'

'Oh, I was just sorting through some cupboards,' said Nan, 'and there it was.' Dad gave the photo to Mum, who looked at it and smiled widely – then handed it to me.

At first I thought it was a photograph of some flares out for a walk. They were massive.

But then I realized someone was actually wearing them . . . Dad.

His hair was very long (far too long) and he was wearing a frilly shirt and a velvet jacket. He also had on a scarf and there was a silver hoop in one ear.

'You weren't in the Dandy Rebels then?' asked Mum.

'What on earth's that?' I grinned.

'My band,' said Dad. 'No, this photo was taken a bit earlier.'

'How old were you?' asked Mum.

'I can't exactly remember,' began Dad.

'I can,' said Nan. 'It was the day of your fifteenth birthday. So exactly thirty years—'

'OK, OK,' interrupted Dad, 'we'll leave it there, I think.'

But it was too late. Elliot was frantically doing some maths in his head, but I knew Dad's age anyway. So then we chorused, 'You're forty-five.'

I added, 'Yeah, Dad, you've hit the big forty-five – you're officially old.'

'All right, don't rub it in,' said Dad quietly.

'Anyway, forty-five is now the new thirty,' said Mum brightly.

'Says who?' demanded Nan.

'All the forty-five-year-olds,' chuckled Grandad. He turned to me. 'Thirty years ago I was complaining about his music. I suppose he does the same to you now.'

'Now that's where you're wrong,' half shouted Dad. 'Just the other day I was watching something on MTV, some rappy stuff, wasn't I, Louis?'

'Were you?'

'Yes, I was. Come on, Louis, back me up here,' said Dad.

'OK, maybe you were for about twenty seconds,' I conceded.

'Well, I had other stuff to do then, but when it was on I was having a boogie.'

'Having a boogie,' I echoed, laughing very loudly. 'No one says that.'

Grandad leaned forward with a teasing smile on his face. 'Face it, son, you're as far away from teenagers today as I am. Well, it happens to every one of us. We all end up as old geezers in the end.' Then he added, 'You're even getting a little paunch just as I did at your age.'

Dad immediately turned to Mum. 'I'm not, am I?'

'Well, maybe just a tiny one,' said Mum.

I'd never seen Dad look more horrified.

Sunday 22 September

8.05 a.m.

Woken up this morning by Dad hissing down my ear, 'How about coming for a run, Louis?'

I thought I was having a nightmare, especially when I blinked up to see a madman bounding about in a baggy tracksuit.

'So what about a run around the block?' asked Dad.

'You go – and then tell me all about it later. Much later,' I added, snuggling down again. 'Try and leave quietly, will you?'

'Oh, come on, Louis, it'll be fun.'

'Trust me, it won't,' I said.

But Dad wasn't going to push off until I agreed. And then he didn't so much run as dance around the block. 'Hey, isn't it great to be up with the lark and be out in the fresh air!' It was foggy and very cold actually. 'We must do this every morning, Louis.'

I couldn't stop shuddering after he'd said that.

'Come on then, I'll race you,' said Dad suddenly. And before I knew it I was in a race.

Dad, for all his prancing about, wasn't a very fast runner. And I overtook him easily. I could hear him panting behind me like a kettle about to explode.

We were almost home and the sound effects from Dad were now alarmingly loud. He was trying his very, very hardest. And he really wanted to win this race. It didn't matter at all to me, but somehow it did to him.

So I slowed up, stumbled a bit and let Dad totter past me.

'Louis, what about that?' he gasped.

'You're just too fast for me, Dad,' I said.

'Ha, ha,' said Dad triumphantly. 'I've still got it.' He reached out to give me a hearty high-five. Instead, he toppled over.

'Hey, Dad . . .'

'No, no, I'm all right,' insisted Dad, heaving himself to his feet. 'It's just my knee. It goes sometimes and it's gone now. Could you . . . ?'

'Lean on me, Dad.'

Dad hobbled home at a speed a geriatric tortoise could have exceeded.

8.30 p.m.

Weirdsville time.

Just after Elliot had gone to bed Mum said, 'We've been meaning to ask you something all weekend. When Rup touched fists with you, he said something . . .'

'Safe,' I said at once.

Mum and Dad both repeated the word.

'And what exactly does it mean?' asked Mum.

'It means you're my mate.'

'But how interesting,' said Mum.

'Extremely,' agreed Dad. 'And could we' – he smiled shyly – 'could we practise touching fists with you now – just so we know the drill.'

I nearly laughed for a week. They were way, way too geriatric to be touching fists.

But I didn't point this out because I'm bigger than that.

So I let Dad try and touch fists with me. And after his first attempt I flinched and said, 'No, no, Dad, you don't whack my knuckles as if we're going to have a big fight. Be a bit more graceful and subtle, like this.'

Mum and Dad watched me really intently, and then they practised touching fists several more times.

'Now you've got it,' I said.

Then Mum asked, 'What about w-i-c-k-e-d. Do you still say that?'

'Yeah, but not how you said it, Mum, all stretched out. No, you've got to say it dead fast – like this.' And I demonstrated.

'Wicked,' said Mum.

'Better,' I said.

'Wicked,' said Dad.

'Perfect,' I said.

Dad beamed.

'And isn't there a little sign you do when you say wicked?' asked Mum.

I grinned. 'There sure is. We'll do it now. I want you both to shake your hands just as if you're flicking water off them.'

Watching my parents say 'wicked' with all the gestures was just wrong on so many levels. But the curtains were tightly drawn – and they were so enjoying themselves.

No harm could come from this, could it?

Watching my parents any twiched, with
all the ... on so many
... Crown
and they went so enjoying it sincere.
So how could come near this could it

CHAPTER TWO

Meet Twitchy

Monday 23 September

4.30 p.m.

Recently my parents made me an offer I
couldn't refuse. Let me tell you all about it.

At my last school I didn't get on with
the headmaster and most of the teachers
– although I made some top mates. So my
parents said I could take a pop at learning
at a completely different school, if I wished.
I wished, all right.

So I had a little gap between schools when
I had a tutor – a resting actor called Todd
who I really liked – and now I've spent two

weeks at my new school. And I don't get on with the headmaster, or most of the teachers, and I haven't made a single mate either.

My new school is much smaller than my last one. I liked the idea of that. It'll be really friendly, I thought. I couldn't have been more wrong. Instead, everyone went berserk at me the second I arrived – and for the most mind-rottenly stupid reason you've ever heard.

When I went to this funny little shop to get fitted for my new uniform, they didn't have my size in stock. But no problem; for now, I'd just go on wearing my hideous old blazer. Well, if I'd worn a Man United scarf when out with a gang of Man City fans I couldn't have got more hassle.

I'd just walked through the gate when this girl dashed up to me, pointing and snarling, 'I hate that school. Everyone there is so stuck-up.'

'No they're not—' I began.

'You all think you're better than everyone else. Well, you're not.'

Soon everyone was crowding around, demanding to know why I was parading about in an enemy uniform. Talk about a lot

23

of fuss about nothing. I mean, all uniforms are equally gross, aren't they? So who cares which one you're wearing? But that's a minority opinion at this establishment.

I only made one person laugh all day. This girl was saying to her friend, 'That sun's too hot.'

'Well, don't touch it,' I shouted.

The girl laughed, then she told me her name was Holly and she's a year older than me. She said, 'People here are not usually so unfriendly.'

'No, it's my fault,' I said, 'for being new.'

She laughed again.

Later, I rang Theo, my best mate from my old school. He said everyone there was really missing me. Correction – he said everyone was really missing me acting stupid. 'You just had to walk into a classroom for people to start laughing.'

'Not here,' I said. 'Here they just want to throw things when they see me.'

And that night I told my parents I wanted to swap schools again and go back to the one I'd just left.

They had a good old laugh at first, thinking

I was joking, and then Dad said, 'But you picked this school.'

And Mum said, 'Got to give it a chance, love.'

I realize it's no use asking them again for a bit. They just won't take me seriously. But I'm not staying here much longer, especially after what's happened today.

At break time I did an impression of our maths teacher who talks through his nose and is always saying, 'No, I'm not having this,' and dribbling while he says it. I did such a wicked impression of him – with some top-class dribbling.

But no one even smiled. And finally this girl said, 'I hate people who are always showing off.'

She really knew how to wound.

And no way am I a show-off! No, I'm an un-discovered comedy icon, which is something totally different, isn't it? But I was so depressed by that insult I called Maddy immediately.

She said maybe I was trying too hard to make people laugh and added, 'People just have to discover you for themselves. So, let them find you in their own time.' She's also coming round to help me sort out my other current big problem.

Tomorrow's history test.

7.45 p.m.

Maddy and I have just reached a unanimous decision.

As I still haven't done any revision, I shouldn't re-sit the history test tomorrow. Especially as this time my parents will undoubtedly hear of my low marks and news like that could set them right back into their bad old boring ways. After all, it was only at the start of September that they'd agreed to let me have my TV and DVD player back in my bedroom. (They'd sneakily removed it one day without my permission.)

So I have no choice but to be ill tomorrow.

But which illness?

I was rather keen on a twenty-four-hour weak heart. 'Just let me lie here with the TV controls beside me,' I'd say with a noble smile. 'My heart will be strong again soon.'

But Maddy said it was much better to stick to that old reliable – a stomach bug. 'You can't go wrong with that!'

She's right, as usual.

9.15 p.m.

Dad was late home again tonight, but before he'd even finished his tea he was firing more questions at me. He said, 'When I said I was having a boogie on Sunday, you laughed.'

I laughed again.

'So no one says that?' asked Dad.

'Not even Shaun the Sheep,' I replied.

'So what would you say if you were off to hear some jolly good catchy music?' said Mum, joining in.

'Well, you might say, *I'm grooving down to some fat tunes,*' I replied.

Mum actually wrote that down in her notebook.

Then Dad said, 'It's so easy to slide into becoming stodgy and out of touch.'

'It can happen to anyone,' went on Mum.

'So,' said Dad, 'we'd like you to tell us what the word on the street is.'

'Any street in particular?' I smiled, though I knew what he meant.

'Just tell us some more of the current hip words—' said Dad.

'Ones young people are using?' I interrupted.

'The young and the youngish,' said Dad briskly. 'Now, what about *Yo* – when exactly do you say that?'

'Just look on me as the Yoda of cool stuff,' I said. 'And harken to my deep wisdom.'

After 'Yo', we moved on to 'my blood' and 'my homies' and tons more of them. I was surprised they were so interested. I suppose it helped them forget they're so ancient. Anyway, I sweated myself to the bone educating them. I am just so good to my parents. ·

Tuesday 24 September

8.30 a.m.

Here's my top tip for faking illness – you've got to prepare for it very carefully. You can't just jump downstairs and announce you're ill. No, a lot of work is needed first.

Like smearing your cheeks with talcum powder to get exactly the right pale look, and dabbing a damp towel over your hair to make it seem all clammy and sweaty.

Then, when you finally totter to the breakfast table, don't say a word – just slump there dead quietly, really underplaying your part.

I waited for Mum to bustle in with my tea and toast. Now, normally I scoff it right down, but today I merely nibbled at it once or twice and then kept pushing it away as if I couldn't bear to even look at it. I also pretended not to notice Mum and Dad sneaking glances at me.

'It's the history test you've been revising so hard for today, isn't it?' said Mum.

'That's right, Mum,' I said faintly, before giving her a shaky smile.

'You haven't got long to eat your breakfast, you know,' said Dad to me at last.

I put my toast down. 'Just not hungry today.'

Then Mum asked the question I'd been waiting for so patiently. 'Are you all right, love?'

I let out a low moan before shooting to my feet. 'Actually, Mum, I think I'm going to be sick.' Then I tore upstairs to the bathroom and locked the door.

I could hear Mum, Dad and Elliot thundering after me. I started making loud throwing-up noises and then turned on every tap as if I were frantically washing it all away.

'Are you all right?' called Mum through the door.

'Oh, yeah,' I croaked. 'Just been a little bit sick.'

I decided to throw in a few more sound effects here. I'd recently watched a cat being sick (surprisingly fascinating), so I was able to add in a startlingly good impression of that.

'Let us in, Louis,' said Dad, sounding really worried now. I did, while still carefully wiping imaginary globules of sick from my nose, my mouth and even my ears and hair. I was so living the part.

'Where's the sick?' asked Elliot, jumping up and down excitedly. 'Oh, please let me see the sick.'

'No, Elliot, go downstairs now and finish your breakfast,' said Mum. 'How long have you been feeling ill, Louis?'

'My stomach hurt all night actually.'

'You do look a bit hot and sweaty,' said Mum.

'And very pale,' murmured Dad.

It was good to see my earlier work so

appreciated. Then, in a thin, quivery voice I whispered, 'If I could just let my stomach rot quietly somewhere, I'm sure I'll feel much better.'

So I'm lying on my bed now and I really think I've got away with it.

But I'm shattered.

I tell you, pretending to be ill really takes it out of you.

12.45 p.m.

What a top morning.

Mum had to leave for work at half-past nine. Having tucked me up in bed, she said she'd ring to see how I was later. So I've got the whole house to myself. And I haven't wasted a single second. I've updated my book of jokes, watched episodes of *Fawlty Towers* and *Porridge*, as well as Michael McIntyre's latest DVD. You see, I'm not content to rest on my comedy laurels. No, I want to be even funnier. So I'm spending as much time as I can in the company of comedy geniuses.

That's why I then read the first chapter of *The Inimitable Jeeves* by P. G. Wodehouse. My tutor, Todd, had introduced me to him.

And he's just the funniest writer in the world. I've been raving about him so much Maddy has even started reading some of the Jeeves stories too.

After all that studying, I raided the biscuit tin and then began flicking through the TV channels. That's when I came across *A Problem Shared*.

If you've seen it, you'll know it's total rubbish. This guy with a face like a ferret and a dodgy perm invites you to share your problems with him. Dr Magnus, he's called.

Some people are there in the studio with him, but others ring in about how they haven't got any friends because of chronic dandruff or something. Dr Magnus will say something totally useless and stupid like, 'But you must learn to make friends with your dandruff,' while smiling right at the camera.

I'd have switched over fast if they hadn't been asking for callers. And when the number went up on the screen – well, I found myself dialling it, didn't I?

I only rang for a laugh, never for a second expecting to get through. But I did – right away (this shows you how popular Dr Magnus is). Before I knew what was going on I was chatting to this soft-voiced girl researcher.

After I'd told her my name, she asked, 'What problem would you like to share with Dr Magnus, Louis?'

I should have just put the phone down then. But that seemed a bit tame. So instead I said with a little sob, 'You won't laugh if I tell you my problem, will you?' (I still hadn't a clue what I was going to say.)

'Of course not, Louis,' she said, so gently that I felt a bit ashamed. But then I thought of phoney Dr Magnus and burst out, 'You know how people at school have nicknames? I've got one that I really hate.'

'Would you like to share it with me?' she cooed.

'All right, it's . . . Twitchy. I'm also known as "The Twitcher" and "Twitty" and sometimes "Twitchy the Twitty Twitcher". But mainly just "Twitchy". The reason is that every so often my face shakes, and a couple of seconds later my whole face just twitches. I'll do it at school or when I'm in the town – anywhere. People often stop and watch me. They even follow me about. And wherever I go I hear them call – "Hey, Twitchy".'

I was having the time of my life making up all this total rubbish. But then the researcher asked if she could take my number and call me back. I thought she was just looking for a way to ring off. Well, I'd had a laugh. So I forgot about it until my phone rang.

It was the researcher again. She asked me some more questions (such as why I wasn't at school) and then said, 'Louis, we'd really like to discuss your interesting problem with Dr Magnus *on air*. Do you feel able to do that?'

I knew I should stop the whole thing now. But it was those two magic words she'd used . . .

And no, I don't mean *Dr Magnus*.

OK, I'd be talking about a totally imaginary problem on one of the worst TV shows ever – but still, I was going to be *ON AIR*.

1.30 p.m.

The next time this friendly researcher rang, it was to tell me to wait on the line as I was the next caller.

I had the phone to my ear while watching

the television. And there on the screen, along-side Dr Magnus in a shiny suit chatting to someone in the audience, were the words: NEXT CALLER, LOUIS, 12, FROM HERTS.

My name was on the telly. I just felt so proud. Next I was counted down. 'Thirty seconds until you're on air . . . twenty seconds until you're on air . . . ten . . .' until down the phone came Dr Magnus's voice, all chummy as if we were old mates. 'Hello there, Louis. Now, you've got an interesting problem. In your own time tell us all about it.'

So I was off, reciting again my completely imaginary life as Twitchy. I added some new stuff like a trip to the cinema when this guy suddenly nudged me and said, 'Can you stop twitching as you're putting my girlfriend off the film?'

'Well, I just can't stop twitching,' I said in a low, mournful voice, 'so in the end I had no choice – I had to vacate the cinema.' Some of the audience went 'Aaah' here. 'It's OK,' I said bravely. 'The DVD will be out fairly soon, I'm sure.' Then, to liven things up a bit, I suddenly gasped. 'Dr Magnus, I've just twitched now.'

'That's quite all right, Louis. I can help you.'

He was dead smooth and confident. 'I believe,' he went on, 'that your twitching is stress-related. So what I want you to do, Louis, is relax and take a deep breath for me, right now.'

I took the deepest, loudest breath the world has ever heard. And from amongst the audience I could hear a few giggles.

'How does that feel?' asked Dr Magnus.

'Truly fantastic,' I said, 'but I've just twitched again. I'll tell you one thing which does relax me, Dr Magnus – telling jokes. Could I tell you one now, please?'

'Er, yes, all right,' he said, a bit taken aback for the first time. 'Provided it's not too long.'

Well, I was off then, wasn't I? And my first joke got such a terrific laugh from the audience in the studio I nearly passed out with joy. I totally forgot about Dr Magnus and what I was on air to talk about and just rattled off joke after joke. Before the audience had stopped laughing at one of my jokes, I was on to the next one.

I was on fire, until finally Dr Magnus bellowed down the line, 'Louis, that's enough!'

I yelled back, 'But guess what! I'm not twitching any more, Dr Magnus. You've cured me. You're a brilliant man – and a brave one too, with a hairstyle like that.'

Dr Magnus said very quietly, 'Well, Louis, you've certainly regained your confidence. We'll be back with a different problem after this brief commercial break.'

But just before the adverts I spotted Dr Magnus shaking his clipboard about in a highly menacing fashion. I bet he'd have loved to fling it at me. Then he vanished, and the line went dead too.

But I didn't care about any of that. I'd got an audience really laughing. I was just bursting with happiness until I heard a voice behind me say, 'Louis, I'm very disappointed in you.'

I whirled round to see Mum standing in my bedroom doorway. She wasn't due back for ages either. But apparently she'd just popped back to see how I was. Talk about sneaky.

I stared at her for a moment, and then blinking my eyes furiously burst out, 'Mum, is that you? What's just happened? I haven't been talking in my sleep again, have I?'

1.35 p.m.

Unfortunately despite my top acting Mum

wasn't buying that one. I've been told to get dressed, and when Dad comes home they're going to have a 'little talk' with me.

7.15 p.m.

I've just been summoned downstairs for my 'little talk' with Mum and Dad. Only they didn't seem anywhere near as furious as I'd expected.

Mum said, 'I know what happened today, Louis. You wanted to do well in your exam not just for yourself, but to please us both as well. Am I right?'

Well, in a way she was right. So I nodded extremely cautiously.

'But on the day of the exam you became so worried about not being good enough, you faked an illness – then acted silly on the phone just to let off some steam.'

Acted silly! I was getting laughs, and nothing in the world's more important than that. But I didn't argue. I was liking the deeply mellow tone Mum was adopting. I might be about to get away with this.

'We want you to know that we will be proud of you whatever mark you get,' said Mum.

But did that include 4%? If it did, my problem was solved. But I had a horrible feeling it didn't.

'So, no worrying and no pressure, all right, Louis?' said Dad, speaking for the first time.

'Yeah, right, cheers,' I said.

I was just so relieved by how it was all going until Mum added, 'I've rung up your school.'

'Oh, have you?' I said, desperately trying to keep my voice light and unconcerned.

'Don't worry, I didn't give you away,' said Mum. 'I let your school think you'd been unwell today, but I also said you wanted to do the history exam tomorrow.'

'You said that, did you?' I gasped. 'You know me too well, Mum.'

'So I've arranged for you to sit the exam tomorrow morning.'

'You're just too good to me,' I quavered.

'Now, if I were you I wouldn't do any more revision tonight,' said Dad. 'Try and forget everything you've learned . . .'

That wouldn't take long.

'Until the morning,' said Dad.

'I'll try,' I said.

'Then you'll be fresh, won't you?' Then he

added, 'You had us both very worried this morning, you know, so no more pretending to be sick, all right?'

'Although,' said Mum with a little smile, 'if you'd said you'd had a sick time – that would have meant you'd had a really great time, wouldn't it?'

'Yo, Mum,' I said, 'you are becoming the Queen of Cool. But how do you know that?'

'Did some research on the internet,' she said proudly.

'Well, Mum,' I said, 'I'm loving your enthusiasm.'

'Found out quite a few new words too,' said Mum. And I let her try every one of them out on me.

Anything to change the subject from history exams.

8.15 p.m.

I told Maddy about me telling jokes on Dr Magnus's show. And afterwards the phone line went oddly quiet.

'Look, I know the show is pants—' I began.

'It's not that,' interrupted Maddy. 'It's just that I'm your agent, so I'm the one who should be getting you work like that. You'll be sacking me soon.'

I laughed at the very idea.

Maddy's my agent and best friend all rolled into one. She's a very easy person to overlook, which is why most people do just that. She's very tall and very shy and looks extremely serious, especially when she sits with her hands folded in her lap, which she does a lot. But the real Maddy is actually funny, and quite pretty too. In fact, there are times when she can look very pretty. For instance, when— but you don't want to know about that, do you?

So anyway, back to our conversation. Maddy said, 'Maybe a big TV executive heard you on Dr Magnus?'

'Yeah, maybe,' I said doubtfully. 'But the thing is, Maddy, I'm getting so sick of waiting.'

'But it will happen. It's got to happen.' I love hearing her say this because she always says it so confidently. 'And very soon now you'll be headlining at some big comedy festival,' she went on. 'The only thing is, you'll have to do at least five encores.'

'Oh, I'll always be very generous with my encores. And then I suppose I'm off to a film premiere.'

'That's right,' said Maddy, 'and all the reporters will be crowding around and pestering you with questions like, "Is it true they're making your life into a cartoon?"'

'And is it true, Maddy?' I asked.

'But of course,' she said. 'Pixar have just bought the rights to your life story, haven't they?'

'Of course they have,' I said, sighing happily.

The present might not be great – but what a future I've got.

Wednesday 25 September

10.45 a.m.

They made me *re-sit* the exam in the hall, just as we had done a week before. But now there were only two of us, me and another guy who'd been away for nearly two weeks.

I watched him writing away with his tongue sticking out the whole time. I sort of envied him being able to write so much. In fact, he made me feel like a right under-achiever. I wished I was clever, or at least knew something about the eighteenth century. What do you bet that boy gets something like 90% at least?

Still, could he have entertained Dr Magnus's audience so lavishly yesterday? And has he got a collection of over one thousand jokes? I think not.

There still remained the problem of this history exam though. Would I even get 4% this time?

But then inspiration struck. I decided to write the examiner a letter.

Here it is.

Dear Examiner,

I have finished your history exam already. Now don't be insulted if I say I didn't like it very much. The questions just weren't for me. But I know you tried your best. Anyway, I'm sure you must get very bored marking paper after paper, so to cheer you up, how about adding on one or two marks for each of my jokes which makes you laugh. Is that a deal?

Great, well here goes:

Q) What did his parents say to the boy ghost?
A) *Spook when you're spooken to.*

Q) Why did the Scout feel dizzy?
A) *Because he did so many good turns.*

Q) Why did the golfer take an extra pair of socks?
A) *In case he got a hole in one.*

Q) Why was the broom late?
A) *It over-swept.*

Altogether, I sent the examiner over forty top jokes like those. A magnificent effort, if I say so myself.

Worth a pass, at least.

Mum trying to be cool

CHAPTER THREE

The Big Stink

Thursday 26 September

8.40 a.m.

DISASTER.

And before school had even started as well.

I rolled up in my new blazer, which Mum had picked up yesterday. I squirmed around in it, but for once the guys in my class actually spoke to me. It was as if I was in the right war paint at last, so now I could join their tribe.

I still didn't intend to hang around this school very much longer, and was mad keen to re-join Theo and all my mates at my old school, but I kind of liked being accepted a little bit too.

And they were all examining my blazer (despite the big wait, it still didn't fit very well) when suddenly this boy grabbed hold of my grey jumper and started killing himself laughing.

'Look, look!' he yelled at the others. I hadn't a clue what he was getting so excited about.

'How old are you?' yelled one boy at me. 'Three?'

'Poor ickle boy,' shouted another. 'Is he frightened of losing his new jumper?'

And then I realized what had happened. Totally unbeknown to me, Mum had sewn a little label at the top of my jumper with my name on it. I could feel my ears burning bright red with shame. But I knew I mustn't react. I had to act as if nothing had happened.

So I just smiled cheerily at everyone and said, 'That nametag does come with its own handy sick bag.' (The best I could think of then.) Then I tore off to the loo and ripped off my name just as fast as I could.

10.30 a.m.

Of course, everyone's still going on about it, asking me if I've got labels sewn onto my socks and pants as well. I gritted my teeth and grinned wildly. I also sent Mum a highly indignant text.

11.00 a.m.

Mum has just replied to my text. She said she was only trying to be helpful and thought labelling my grey jumper would help keep track of it when I got changed for PE. My mum is such an innocent.

11.25 a.m.

Just when I thought my day couldn't get any worse I was sent to see Mr Morgan, the headmaster.

Now, being asked to drop in on the headmaster can mean only one thing – you're in deep poo.

But what have I done wrong? Nothing sprang to mind. Perhaps he'd heard about me having my name sewn into my jersey and wanted to tell me this isn't the behaviour he expected? I smiled a little then. But as I plodded up the long, winding staircase to his lair, I don't mind admitting my stomach was twisting about very anxiously.

I was admitted at once into his throne room. There he was, sitting behind the desk – a large man in an expensive suit. He had a very lined, crumpled face with tiny eyes and a permanent smile. Only he had no lips to speak of (so I shan't mention them again) and his smile wasn't so much friendly as deeply eerie. I tell you, he looked more like a Bond villain than most Bond villains – Dr Sinister is what I'd call him.

Dr Sinister just sat studying me as if I were some mysterious parcel he'd received and he was now trying to guess what was inside. Then he slapped my history exam paper down onto his desk so loudly he made me jump. 'Anything you'd like to tell me about this?' he demanded.

I said, 'Well, I don't think I got top marks. Did I get any marks?'

'You were given the chance to take this exam again after your atrocious first attempt and this is what you come up with . . .'

Then he started reading aloud the jokes I'd

written at the end of the exam paper. I tell you, if he ever decides to change his career, he's got no chance as a comedian. For a start, he has no idea how to time a joke. I didn't feel this was the moment to offer him some tips though.

Then he asked, 'Have you anything to say before I ring your parents?' That brought an instant horror alert. My parents have been behaving so much better lately. But his phone call could send them hurtling right back to their pushy parent ways. I had to think of something fast.

'Flashbacks,' I shouted out desperately.

'Flashbacks?' he purred.

'Yeah, I get flashbacks in exam rooms – ever since I was attacked by a plague of killer wasps. There was a wasps' nest right above my head and everyone got evacuated to safety – except me. The doctor said he'd never seen an attack like it. I suppose I'm lucky to be alive at all, really. And sometimes when I'm sitting in an exam room I get flashbacks. That's what happened yesterday. I had this really massive flashback.'

I like saying the word 'flashback' (as you

might have noticed). In fact, I nearly said it again until I saw the headmaster's face. They say when leopards are about to spring at you they get a certain look in their eyes. That's exactly what I saw then in Dr Sinister's eyes.

Then he leaped to his feet while breathing loudly through his nose. I was about to get a truly massive rollicking. But instead, he broke wind with such force it actually made my hair blow. And it let off a smell that could stun a zebra.

I tell you, if they gave out Olympic prizes for farting, my headmaster would be right up there on the podium.

Of course, he couldn't admit he'd let one go and have a bit of a chuckle about it. Instead, he tried to pretend nothing had happened, while at the same time hotfooting it to the window and opening it as wide as it would go.

'Your incredible story—' he began. He stopped and got out his hankie and started coughing into it.

I felt hot and began to shake – I so wanted to explode into laughter. But instead I joined in the coughing. Suddenly he sped forward, practically threw my exam paper at me and said, 'You will re-do this paper at home tonight, supervised by your parents. I shall expect a note signed by them saying this has been done under exam conditions and it will be handed in by nine o'clock tomorrow.'

I gaped at him. He hadn't believed a single word of my story. But right now he just wanted to get shot of me and cover the room in air freshener.

Before I left I asked helpfully, 'Shall I leave the door open, sir?'

'Just go,' he spluttered.

As soon as I was outside I laughed so much I got hiccups.

12.30 p.m.

At lunch time I heard this voice behind me say, 'Hey, Louis.'

It was Holly, the girl who'd laughed at my joke that first day. We'd gone on chatting occasionally ever since.

'It *was* you, wasn't it?' she asked.

'Probably.' I thought she was going to ask

about that wretched nametag on my jumper.

But instead she said, 'I was off sick on Tuesday, and there on Dr Magnus's show was this boy called Louis, from Herts, who sounded just like you. He was talking all about his head twitching.' She smiled. 'It's not twitching now.'

I grinned. 'Dr Magnus cured me.'

'And how on earth did you get on that show?' she asked.

'I just rang up,' I said.

'And made up all that rubbish?'

'Talking rubbish comes easily to me.' I laughed.

'I couldn't believe it when I saw your name up there.'

'I'm a boy full of surprises,' I said.

Then she called over to two other girls, 'Yeah, it was him.' Turning back to me, she said very quickly, 'We'll see you at the school disco on Saturday then.'

I hesitated. I'd heard about it but hadn't really thought of going. 'Probably not,' I said.

'Look, don't let the dorks in your class put you off.'

She'd called the boys in my class dorks. I was liking Holly more and more.

'You've every right to go there, haven't you?'

'Yeah,' I agreed, and then added, 'I suppose I might look in – provided I can control my twitching, of course.'

Holly grinned. 'I fell out of bed laughing when I heard you on there. See you on Saturday then.'

4.00 p.m.

Maddy said they're well into the eighteenth century in history at her school. So if I bring the exam paper round to her tonight she'll give me all the right answers. Then I only have to copy them out when I'm doing the exam at home later.

She really is a top agent.

9.20 p.m.

I've just finished my exam. Mum and Dad had been timing me. They piled into my bedroom when the time was up.

'How was that?' asked Mum, all concerned. 'You should have told us you weren't feeling well enough yesterday to take it then. It's so good of your headmaster to let you have a fair mark by doing it again!' (Obviously, I'd had to let on that I'd been sick again yesterday but hadn't wanted to let them down . . .)

'Did you have enough time?' asked Dad.

'Just about,' I said. Actually, I'd finished copying down Maddy's answers yonks ago.

'Any idea of how you think you've done?'

'I think I've done OK,' I said modestly.

They both beamed at me.

Then Dad said, 'So your mum says you're going to hit the school disco on Saturday.'

'Well, I thought I'd liven things up,' I said.

'I'll give you a lift there and pick you up afterwards,' went on Dad.

'Hey, Dad, thanks.'

'Hope it rocks,' said Dad with a big smile. 'And you hear some fat tunes.'

'And you have a sick time,' added Mum.

My mum and dad crack me up. And I'm sure if I recorded them and then put it on YouTube they'd be comedy gold.

But I'd never do that to them.

Friday 27 September

8.30 a.m.

Every day Dad has taken this battered old briefcase to work – until today. Now he's got a flash new bag with a sports logo, and he slings it over his shoulder.

'Hey, Dad, you look almost cool,' I said. Then I noticed something else. 'You've forgotten your tie – have a double detention.'

Dad grinned. 'First day ever I've gone to work tie-less. But Rup and his associates never wear a tie and you've got to keep up, haven't you? Anyway, have a sick day, Louis. Laters.'

I was kind enough not to laugh. I even felt a bit sorry for him. Poor old Dad, trying to keep up. A bit of a shame really that it's hopeless. He'll always be old and past it now.

3.30 p.m.

My exam paper has been marked already. I passed this time with a truly dazzling 65%. I just feel so proud.

5.20 p.m.

Now Holly wants to friend me on Facebook.
So do three other girls in her year. Could my
days as the school's social outcast be over?

Dad thinks he's _so_ cool but he's NOT

CHAPTER FOUR

Dad Looks for 'His Blood'

Saturday 28 September

5.30 p.m.

One of a parent's most important functions is buying you the very latest trainers. This should be done at least once a year – preferably twice. What you never expect to see is parents buying the very latest trainers for *themselves*. But that's what I've just witnessed. I watched them prancing about the house in their big, chunky new white trainers.

'You know, they're actually quite comfortable,' said Mum. 'We really bought them to wear at the gym.'

'You're going to a gym now!' I said.

'And why shouldn't we?' said Dad. 'We've just enrolled.'

'Now I read somewhere,' said Mum, 'that today people are wearing trainers with the tongues out.'

But not people in their riper years like my parents. If they did that outside they'd just be exposing themselves – and me – to ridicule. I breathed heavily for a second until I remembered something.

How many times had Dad gone out running? Once. What do you bet Dad and Mum only go the gym once too? And it'll be pretty dark when they leave as well. So with a bit of luck no one will see them. Then this little fad will be over and Dad will return to his normal, shabby trainers, while these new trainers will languish in a cupboard somewhere – unused and forgotten. Actually, Dad's trainers might fit me soon . . .

So then I showed him exactly how young people are wearing their trainers today – with the tongues out and the laces undone.

'Now we're really chilling,' said Dad.

'Oh yeah, you sure are.' I grinned.

6.00 p.m.

I've just rung Maddy and ever so casually asked what she was doing tonight.

'My mum's best friend has recently moved to the area,' she said, 'and she's coming round tonight with her son, Edgar, who I've got to entertain.'

'You've never mentioned him,' I said.

'Well, I haven't seen him for years,' said Maddy. 'But Mum wants me to be extra nice to him as he hasn't got many friends.'

'That sounds like fun,' I murmured. But secretly I was very disappointed. You see, I'd planned to ask Maddy if she wanted to go to the disco with me. I didn't ask her before, because she doesn't go to my school and wouldn't know anyone. But then *I* go to my school and don't really know anyone either. So we'd both be in the same boat really.

Now I was very annoyed I hadn't mentioned it to her before. For if I was with Maddy tonight and no one spoke to me apart from Holly and her mates, it wouldn't matter at all. Maddy and I would have had a laugh anyway. But without her . . .

Do you know I nearly asked Maddy to

change her plans? But then I decided that would have sounded a bit desperate and intense, almost as if I were asking her out or something. Ha, ha, ha. The very idea.

9.05 p.m.

(Q) *What's the very worst place to hold a disco?*
(A) *A school hall.*

I mean, this is where they hold assemblies and make us do exams. So, the very centre of pupil torture. And just because they've stuck up a glitter ball and shoved on some music doesn't make it somewhere else.

Especially as the first things you see when you arrive are the chairs for Monday's assembly all stacked up in the corner. The smell of the school – a mixture of disinfectant, polish and misery – still lingers over everything too.

And that's not even mentioning the teachers. OK, they might be slinking about in their casual jackets and not quite so sensible shoes, but no one wants to meet them at a party or anywhere else on a Saturday night, to be honest.

No wonder everyone's just hanging around the edges of the hall in unfriendly little clusters. The middle of the hall where we're all supposed to be wildly dancing and – whisper this – enjoying ourselves, is completely empty.

The only highlight is a very long table of food. But even this is overseen by beady-eyed teachers. One handing me another plate of food asked, 'Is this seconds or thirds, Louis?'

'It's fifths, actually,' I said.

As for Holly – yeah, she did come over with three of her mates to chat with me about going on Dr Magnus's show. They were dead fascinated for all of two minutes. Then they all clomped away again. Later, I saw Holly with this Year Nine boy who kept strutting about as if he thought he was really cool. While the guys in my class all just gawped at me as if I'd got three heads or something.

Then one boy in my class shouted out at me, 'I thought you'd be with your posh mates from your old school.'

There was no point in arguing that none of my old mates were remotely posh. I just gave him a very cool smile and then strolled off again.

Some of my classmates called out other stuff to me, none of which sounded remotely friendly. But I've decided to just smile and take everything they say as a compliment. So if they say, 'You're a total idiot,' I'll merely grin and reply, 'Thank you, you're too kind.' Don't ever let them know they've got to you, even if they have.

It's weird really how you can be shut away in your bedroom and feel far less lonely than here surrounded by people. In fact, I've never felt more cut-off and out of the loop anywhere than here.

I shouldn't have come, should I?

Already this party seems to have lasted longer than the Hundred Years War – see, I do know some history! And Dad wasn't picking me up until half-past ten at the earliest. I decided to text him to come now.

I very nearly did that, but then I decided no, I won't do that, as that would mean all the dorks, as Holly calls them, have won. I'll stick this out somehow.

Want to know what I'm doing right now?

I'm strolling about with a truly massive plate of food and looking as if I've just heard the best joke in the world. And I've lost count of how often I've wished Maddy was here with me.

10.45 p.m.

It was time for Dad to pick me up and I was about to slink off outside when someone actually came up and spoke to me. I nearly fell over with shock, as I was certain I'd become invisible hours ago.

It was a girl with a heavy cold, who between sniffs asked me if it was true I'd been interviewed on a TV show this week.

I told her all about it, and then she asked if I was going to be on any future television shows.

'Negotiations are in progress, but they're kind of top-secret. I'm leaving it to my agent to sort out.'

'You've got an agent!' she gasped.

'Oh yeah, sure,' I said with bewitching casualness.

'But you're at school.'

'Yeah, I am, but school is actually a very small part of my life. I'm mainly involved in the comedy industry, and I'm looking to diversify into lots more television shows.'

She paused here to blow her nose – but in a highly impressed way. I then asked her if she would like a spare hankie. She said she really would as her cold was getting worse and worse. So I donated my very cleanest one.

'And don't bother to return it,' I said. 'It's yours, and now every time you blow your nose you can think of me.'

She laughed and said, 'I can see you on TV.' Then she had to put her head right back as she thought she might be getting a nosebleed.

'My colds often bring on nosebleeds,' she announced.

'You're certainly having a busy night,' I said.

OK, her health could be better, but now I feel as if I've made a new friend. That nosebleed never materialized so now I'm getting Julie (yeah, she even told me her name: things are getting serious) a drink.

More soon.

11.00 p.m.

I'd just handed Julie her drink when the lights went on and the teachers announced

64

the disco was over, which was a bit of a shame. The teachers also asked for volunteers to help clean up. So immediately everyone – including Julie and me – just stampeded out of the hall.

We were all surging outside towards the car park when a voice shouted out of the darkness, 'Yo, everyone, hope you had a wicked time. But I'm looking for my blood. Is he here?' Instantly an eerie silence settled on everyone – although if you'd listened really hard you'd have heard my skin crawling.

Everyone just gaped open-mouthed at this middle-aged man in brand-new trainers, capering about in front of them.

Julie giggled and whispered, 'Gross or what.'

I didn't answer. I couldn't. I'd just been shocked out of my brain.

'Who do you think he is?' she asked. 'Is he someone's dad?'

I didn't need to fill her in on this one, for then Dad spotted me. 'Yo, Louis, there you are, dude.'

This isn't really happening, I told myself. *I've slipped into a parallel universe for a few moments.*

'Hope you've been having fun with your homies.' My dad was going off his onion right in front of my entire school. That was the only explanation I could think of.

'He's not your dad, is he?' whispered Julie to me. She couldn't have sounded more shocked if I'd told her my parents were Martians.

'He'll be fine when he's had his bedtime story,' I said, in a desperate attempt to make her laugh. It didn't work.

Stunned as I was, I knew one thing for certain. I had to get Dad away from here, fast. So in three giant strides I reached him, put my arm around him and then bundled him out of the school gates. I tell you, a superhero couldn't have moved more nippily.

I didn't say a word to him either. I knew I had to remain strong and silent until I had escorted Dad right away from the crime scene.

As I was escorting Dad away, my stunned classmates finally came to life. A whole group yelled out 'Yo' to my dad. Totally unaware that they were making fun of him again, Dad yelled back, 'Yo, keep it real, guys.'

Everyone fell about laughing – except me.

What had got into Dad tonight? Previously when he'd given me a lift after a party, he'd just waited silently in the car. Not saying a single word to me until we'd driven right away, and if I had any friends with me, keeping conversation to a total minimum even then.

Yet tonight, it was as if he'd had a body swap with a madman. He was a different person. He wasn't even walking like my dad. Instead, he was copying Rup's slouchy walk.

AT LAST we'd reached Dad's car and the question just burst out of me. 'Dad, why, *why* did you go up to the school tonight and . . . and . . . well, why?'

Dad was standing by one side of the car, me the other. And for a second he stood so still he looked like a shadow. Then he started gabbling excitedly.

'Well, I'd parked so far away I was very worried I'd missed you. So in the end I strolled up to the school and took a quick peek inside and saw the disco was still going on. I couldn't spot you anywhere, but do you know the really amazing thing?' Dad moved closer to me, his face glowing. 'Nothing has changed, Louis. *Nothing.* There was still the girl crying on the stairs and her friends all around her, the gate-crashers outside, the boys having a bit of a scuffle . . .'

Behind us two boys shouted, 'Shame!' I knew that was directed at me.

But I don't think Dad even heard them; he was too busy being misty-eyed. 'I was transported right back and the years just fell away from me tonight.'

I was looking at Dad very anxiously now. 'Really?'

'And people can just get stuck in their roles, can't they? Yes, even me.' He edged even closer to me. 'So I thought, tonight I'll break right out of my boring old role and really surprise you and your mates.'

He'd done that, all right.

'I'll show everyone I'm not so far away from them as they might think. And thanks to you teaching your mum and me the current lingo, I had the confidence to do just that.'

THANKS TO ME!!!

Now I know exactly how Dr Frankenstein felt when his creation broke out and went rampaging around the countryside. I'd taught Mum and Dad those words only for their own private use. I never expected them to say such words in public – let alone turn up outside a school disco and yell them out in a voice loud enough to be heard several galaxies away.

'There doesn't have to be this great gap between the generations, does there?' said Dad.

Yes, there does.

'If you have the right attitude and keep up with the latest wicked words, you can slip right back, can't you?'

No, you can't.

Dad could never slip right back. His expiry date was years and years ago. And he can't fight that. It's over for ever for him.

Yet Dad seems to think the 'latest wicked words' are like passwords. Rattle off those and he's back chilling with the young again.

This is a total nightmare.

CHAPTER FIVE

Incredible News

Sunday 29 September

10.00 a.m.

Early this morning I rang Maddy. When I'd finished telling her about Dad's antics last night there was silence.

'Hey, are you still there?' I asked.

'Yes . . .' But her voice seemed to have shrunk.

'I thought you might have de-materialized with shock.'

'No, it's just I don't know what to say to you,' she said.

'That's a first,' I said.

'I mean, your mum sewing your name on your jersey is gross, but what your dad did, that's—'

'That's beyond gross,' I interrupted.

'Exactly,' she said. 'What's your dad said today about last night?'

'Oh, he still thinks he was a brilliant success, breaking down the barriers between generations.'

Maddy sighed heavily.

'And I heard him telling Mum in the kitchen that age is only a state of mind.'

'He must be a real worry for you,' said Maddy.

'He is. And that's what you get for doing a good deed,' I said bitterly. 'I sweated myself to the bone teaching my parents all the latest words, trying to brighten up their declining years.'

'I think you've over-stimulated them,' she added. 'Keep your dad right away from your school from now on.'

'I'd put him under house arrest if I could,' I said.

'And keep telling yourself this is just a phase he's going through,' went on Maddy. 'In a few

71

days he'll be just like my dad again – spending his time at garden centres and buying new toolkits and making up pub quizzes.'

'Right now that sounds like paradise,' I said.

Monday 30 September

4.00 p.m.

My popularity has rocketed. I'm now the most popular boy in my school. Everyone wants to be my mate. So many people, in fact, that I've had to put them into teams. There are my Monday mates and my Tuesday mates . . .

ONLY JOKING.

But you guessed that, didn't you?

'I'm looking for my blood,' followed by 'Your dad's so sad,' and 'Your dad's from Planet Weirdo,' were called out the very second I arrived at school. They've swirled around me all day.

You try and laugh it off. That's why I've been laughing loudly and falsely all day. But inside I felt like such a loser. No, make that *two* losers. As now it's as if Dad is trailing around at school beside me. My social life is definitely over. It's just lucky I didn't have any social life in the first place.

As I was leaving school, Julie tapped me on the arm, and in between coughing (wouldn't you know it, her cold's brought on a cough as well now) hissed, 'You've just got to try and forget what your dad did on Saturday night.'

'Yeah, but will anyone else?'

She paused for a long moment and then said finally, 'In a few years' time – maybe.'

6.45 p.m.

Just when I was ready to consign today to the rubbish bin of history something incredible has happened.

Mum and Dad had gone off for their first trip to the gym and Elliot was downstairs watching telly when my mobile rang.

It was a bright, bubbly-sounding girl called Evie. She told me she was the producer of a TV show. 'Maybe you've heard of us. It's called *Kids with Attitude.*'

I hadn't heard of it but I pretended I had. 'Oh yeah, I'm sure I've seen it.'

'We're on the same satellite channel as Dr Magnus.'

'Oh, good old Dr Magnus,' I said.

'We heard you on his show on Tuesday,' said Evie. Then she added with a chuckle, 'How's your twitch?'

'Totally gone,' I said.

We both laughed and then she said, 'We at *Kids with Attitude* were very impressed by your joke-telling. And my associate producer had already been given your details by a big fan of yours – Josie.'

'Oh, Josie,' I said. She was the producer of *Tomorrow's Stars*, which I'd almost appeared on. 'How is she?'

'Oh, very well – so we've had you on file, Louis, but when we heard you on Dr Magnus we thought you might be the very person to help us out.'

I was all attention now.

Evie went on, '*Kids with Attitude* is a weekly talent show, but much edgier than previous ones. We have one winner and one runner-up each week, picked by our studio audience. Then all the winners take part in the All-Winners Final, and we also select one of the runners-up to join in the grand final too. Well, the thing is, one of our scheduled acts on Thursday may have to pull out.' (She didn't say why.) 'This would leave us without a comedian, so we'd like you to be on standby. It may mean calling on you at very short notice.'

'No problemo.'

'And you are happy to be our standby?'

'Well, I'd be happier if I was definitely on the show' – she gave another little chuckle here – 'but yeah, definitely.'

'We'd like you to perform for three minutes.'

'I could do three hours if you wanted.'

'Three minutes is fine,' she said firmly. 'I will be in contact again to let you know if you're needed on Thursday. Thanks so much, Louis. Bye for now.'

Don't let me get too excited, dear diary. That phone call doesn't mean I'm actually going to be on *Kids with Attitude*. This could just be another show I'm *nearly* on. I'm building up quite a collection of those.

But it's still the best news I've had for several centuries.

8.05 p.m.

My parents have just tottered back from the gym. Dad sank down on the couch.

'Been enjoying yourselves, have you?' I grinned.

'It was ... very interesting,' said Mum firmly. 'They monitored our heartbeats and gave us a fitness plan and—'

'And the whole place,' interrupted Dad, 'is overrun by very good athletes – or people who think they're very good athletes – heaving up weights and pounding away on treadmills.'

Mum got up and patted him on the shoulder. 'We said we weren't going to let them intimidate us, didn't we?'

Dad muttered something and looked the grumpiest he had for days. I just knew they wouldn't be returning to that gym any time soon. I also decided this wasn't the moment to tell them about *Kids with Attitude*. Best to wait until it was all confirmed anyway.

There was only one person I would tell now.

9.30 p.m.

I raced round to Maddy's house. Her older

sister Vicky opened the door. 'Another boy to see my sister,' she announced.

I laughed very briefly. What was she talking about? Another boy?

Then Maddy sprang out of the dining room where she often does her homework. 'Oh, hi, Louis,' she hissed. 'This is a surprise.'

'Why are you whispering?'

'Someone's writing a poem in the dining room.'

'Anyone you know?'

Maddy smiled a little nervously. 'Edgar.'

'And why's Edgar writing a poem in your dining room?'

Maddy shrugged. 'He said he wanted somewhere peaceful and quiet.'

At that moment the dining-room door opened, and a smallish boy appeared. He was wearing a shirt which he could have borrowed from his grandad. And I'm sure I'd seen Grandad wearing trousers exactly like those Edgar had on. Even worse, he looked and smelled so disgustingly clean and well-scrubbed. And his shirt was so neatly tucked into his trousers. Only his black curly hair was all tousled, but it looked like he'd messed it up deliberately in a desperate and futile attempt to try and look interesting and artistic.

'Oh, sorry if we disturbed you,' said Maddy. Why was she acting as if he was some little emperor? 'Edgar, this is Louis.'

Edgar lowered his head and peered at me through his hair. 'Ah, so you're him, are you?'

'Last time I checked I was.'

He peered at Maddy. 'I've finished my poem. It was bursting to be expressed.'

'So what's it about?' I asked.

'A light bulb,' he said.

'Quite a bright poem then,' I quipped.

Edgar raised both his eyebrows.

Then Maddy looked at me excitedly. 'Something's happened? You've got news.'

She can always read me like a book. So then I told her all about my phone call. And her face lit up, brighter than a hundred light bulbs.

'Oh, Louis, this could be it!'

'I know.'

'You'll have to practise your jokes over and over.'

'I know again,' I said.

'And I'll make sure you only tell the really funny ones.'

I grinned. 'My agent's word is final.'

'It really is,' agreed Maddy.

'*Kids with Attitude.*' Edgar said the name very slowly, as if he were tasting it. 'No, I don't care for the title at all – it's trying much too hard.'

'We'll have it changed for you then,' I hissed furiously.

'An adult thought up that title for certain. That's why it smells phoney,' said Edgar. 'I never watch television these days, but if you let me know when it's on . . .'

'We'll send you an invitation,' I said.

Edgar raised his eyebrows again before announcing, 'I must take my leave now. I shall take a leisurely walk while savouring all the autumn smells and letting some of Keats's work run about in my head.' Then he turned to me. 'Do you know Keats?'

'Does he play for Spurs?' I grinned. I *had* heard of Keats, actually.

But Edgar sighed. 'Young people's lack of interest in great poets disturbs me greatly.'

He spoke as if he were some learned professor of about ninety. Then he bowed very low as if he were off to take part in a duel, and left.

'He seems . . . horrible,' I exclaimed. 'How do you stand him?'

Maddy just smiled.

'I bet he's popular at school,' I went on.

'He's got a tutor right now as he didn't get on with the boys in his school . . .'

'Well, what a surprise,' I said. 'But here's the really important question – has he got a bit at the back where you can switch him off?'

Maddy smiled again. 'He's not so bad when you get to know him.'

'I'll take your word for that. You know your trouble, Maddy – you're too kind-hearted.'

She just replied briskly, 'Come on then, let me hear your jokes.'

Tuesday 1 October

9.00 p.m.

Kids with Attitude haven't rung yet. I asked Maddy if I should call Evie just in case she's lost my number.

Maddy replied, 'Definitely not – looks far too desperate.'

But I *am* desperate. That's why I'm sleeping with my mobile under my pillow. I know TV people work odd hours. And this is one call I really do *not* want to miss.

Wednesday 2 October

6.45 p.m.

Kids with Attitude have just called.

And it's the best news ever.

I'm on the show tomorrow night.

I tried to hide my excitement and be a bit cool about it all, but Evie could tell all right, and I think she was trying to calm me down as she said, 'Now I must warn you, Louis, this is quite a different talent show to others you might have seen. For a start, the entire audience are teenagers.'

'Great,' I said.

'Yes,' said Evie a bit doubtfully. 'Each teenager is given a tiny trumpet.'

'Do they blow that instead of clapping?' I asked.

'Not exactly,' said Evie. She gave a nervous

cough. 'If they don't like your act they will blow their trumpet. And if enough trumpets sound . . .'

'I have to stop my act.'

'That's right. You are led away, actually.'

A shiver ran down my spine.

'But that doesn't worry you,' said Evie.

'Oh no,' I said. 'I laugh in the face of trumpets. Bring them on, is what I say.'

'I like your confidence,' said Evie. Then she went through the plan for tomorrow. I had to be ready by half-past five. That's when a car would pick me up.

'Hope it's a sports car,' I said. 'I'll only sit in sports cars. Just joking,' I added quickly as I didn't hear Evie laughing. She whizzed through the rest of the arrangements and I knew I should have been listening intently but my head was just buzzing. At the end Evie said, 'And of course you will be accompanied by a parent.'

'Sure. Of course. For certain,' I said. I hadn't told Mum and Dad anything about *Kids with Attitude* yet, but I know they'll be thrilled and proud and excited and probably fighting over who goes with me.

So, no problem there.

But first I shall call Maddy and tell her the news – no, I'll pop round so I can also rehearse my act with her one last time.

7.15 p.m.

I just couldn't believe it. He was there again. Edgar. I realized right away because Maddy was once more whispering outside the dining room.

'Composing another poem, is he? What's it about this time – a plug, or has he moved on to the airing cupboard?'

Maddy lowered her voice even more. 'Right now, Edgar feels as if he's trapped down a well of loneliness and no one can ever hear his voice – except me.' She couldn't help fluttering a bit proudly. And I was – well, to be honest, I was very disappointed in Maddy. That's something I've never written before. But how could she believe all his ear-rotting rubbish. It was so obvious to me he was just a big-headed poser. Why wasn't it obvious to Maddy too?

'Do you want to go in and say hi to him?' she went on.

'I won't actually because I've just had my tea.'

Then she looked at me. 'Have *Kids with Attitude* rung?'

'Of course they have.'

'And what did they—?'

'Well, I wouldn't have come round here to tell you I wasn't going to be on.'

'No, no,' cried Maddy quickly. 'It's just – you looked so angry when you came in.'

This was on account of Edgar cluttering up the place, but I just said, 'No, this is my happy face. Honestly.'

'But this is totally brilliant!' she yelled, which would have been a top moment if she hadn't immediately added, 'Sorry, Edgar.'

Then, so as not to disturb him, we slipped up to Maddy's room, where I practised my act three times. We kept getting interrupted, first by Maddy's mum and then by her sisters. But they all said they'd be glued to the screen tomorrow night.

And when I asked Maddy if she wanted to come along to the show with me, she said, 'Try and stop me.'

'I'm not sure which of my parents will be

coming along,' I said. 'If it's my dad he'll probably try and get up on the stage too – as a very ancient "Kid with Attitude".'

Maddy laughed.

'You think I'm joking,' I said.

8.00 p.m.

I'd never expected this.

My parents have just totally ruined everything.

Dad thinks he's so cool but he's NOT

CHAPTER SIX

'Cool Dad'

Wednesday 2 October (cont'd)

8.25 p.m.

When I got back Elliot was in bed and Mum and Dad were watching television, so I just said, 'Guess what. Someone who's in this room right now will be on your telly tomorrow night.' Then I told them all about Evie's phone calls. After which I said, 'So which lucky parent will be coming with me? Are you going to draw lots or have an arm wrestle?'

Mum said very quietly, 'That's certainly interesting news, Louis.' She got up. 'Your dad and I are just going to have a little talk about it.' Dad got to his feet too.

I told them, 'You needn't worry about saving up for a celebratory present yet, you know. Wait until I've won.'

'We won't be long,' said Mum.

And they weren't. They trooped back from the kitchen again a few minutes later and they were both smiling. That's a good sign, I thought.

Mum said brightly, 'You've had a big upheaval recently, changing schools. Now that can't have been easy, but you're coping with it so well. And we were both thrilled with your history exam result on Friday. But we don't want you to have any more disruptions right now. So we both feel this last-minute TV show, about which we've never heard—'

'It hasn't been on telly very long – that's why you've never heard of it,' I interrupted.

'Well, anyway, the timing is all wrong for you and we're not giving our permission for this one,' said Mum.

'So because I did well in my exam last week I can't go on *Kids with Attitude?*' I cried.

'That's not what we said,' replied Mum. She tried to explain again – and she was doing all the talking. Dad was just sitting beside her, nodding away like one of those nodding dogs you see in the back of cars.

'But this is my big chance,' I said.

'Oh, there'll be many, many more chances,' said Mum breezily.

'You don't know that,' I said. 'And anyway, if I'm not on *Kids with Attitude* tomorrow, it'll mess up the balance of the whole show. They need a comedian.'

Mum totally ignored this. 'I really think our decision is for the best. And one day in the future I know you'll thank us.'

That is one of the most annoying things parents can say – and one of the most patronizing. Really angry now, I snapped, 'You're not the only time-traveller in this family. And I can tell you I'll never thank you for your decision. I'll probably never forgive you either.'

Then I stormed off.

9.05 p.m.

So after Dad ruined my entire social life on Saturday night, he and Mum are going for the double now by robbing me of the best chance I've ever had to be discovered as a comedian.

How are they not getting what a good chance this is for me? All this rubbish about it disrupting my life. Don't they realize I *want* my life disrupted? In fact, I can't wait.

But what can I do?

It's no use arguing with Mum. She's got that determined look on her face. So, how about Dad? He tends to stick with Mum on decisions like this. He won't want to go against her.

But I've just had an idea. It'll mean me being very clever – and lying quite a bit. But it might just work.

It *has* to work.

9.40 p.m.

I've just set my plan into action. First of all, it was essential I saw Dad on his own. So I waited until he was in the kitchen making a pot of tea and then I strolled in.

Dad looked up. 'Calmed down a bit, have you?'

'Oh, yeah,' I lied.

'Not too disappointed about *Kids with Attitude*, are you?'

'No, no,' I lied again.

'Another time, definitely. So, are we still good, dude?'

'Of course we are. In fact, we're just great,' I said, giving a superb impression of a ray of sunshine. 'Anyway, I've got to keep in with my cool dad.'

Dad stood right in front of me. 'What's this?'

'All the guys in my school are talking about you.'

This was true.

'They're all saying how great it was that you could just hang out with everyone at the school gates.'

This was, of course, completely untrue. But Dad believed me instantly and shook his head delightedly and started jumping about in the kitchen like an over-excited seven-year-old. 'I thought it had gone well, but I had no idea they all think I'm cool now. Kind of flattering, I suppose.'

'I was also telling them how you used to be in the Dandy Rebels.'

'You must also tell them,' cried Dad eagerly, 'just what kind of a band we were. New Romantics – a total reaction against the grey austerity of Punk, so we were bursting with bright, flamboyant clothes . . .'

I let Dad bore on for a bit – he was getting more and more worked up – before I cut in, 'I bet the Dandy Rebels would have won *Kids with Attitude* if it had been on in your day.'

'Well you know what, I think we might have done. Back in the day we had quite a following, played at school discos all over the country—'

'And you'd have jumped at the chance of going on a show like that.'

'Oh, for sure, because those sort of chances don't come round very often.' Dad stopped pacing and went very still. 'I've just walked straight into a trap, haven't I?'

'But, Dad, you said yourself those sorts of chances don't come round very often. Your band never got its chance – don't deny me mine.'

Dad frowned. 'Look, Louis, just leave it with me – but I'm not promising anything.'

9.50 p.m.

Now the hard part. Waiting to see if my cunning plan has worked.

91

10.15 p.m.

I was coming out of the bathroom when Dad bounded up the stairs.

'Quick word,' he said, stalking into my bedroom with a conspiratorial smile. He seemed worked up all right – but was it good news? 'Do me a favour,' he said, 'and make sure you're extremely funny tomorrow night, because you are going to be on television.'

'Hey, Dad—!' I started.

But before I could say anything else he went on, 'Your mum took some persuading, I can tell you. And you've got to promise us you won't let your school work suffer. We want lots more of those top marks, Louis.'

'Sure, sure.' I'd have agreed to anything then.

'But we both feel that as these opportunities are very rare' – for a moment he looked wistful and I was sure he was thinking of his band again – 'you should seize hold of this one. More good news. I'll be coming with you tomorrow night.'

'Brilliant. But you know we'll have to leave by half-five.'

'Well, after all my recent late-night meetings

I think I'm allowed one evening when I can come home at a reasonable time,' said Dad.

'And Maddy wants to be there too.'

'Wicked!' cried Dad.

Of course, I winced then. Hearing Dad – hearing any parent – say 'wicked' was against all the laws of the universe. But I have to admit, the way Dad said 'Wicked' was spot-on. He'd got the gesture just right too. I'd taught him so well.

10.30 p.m.

I was feeling really happy with how I'd turned things around until I rang Maddy.

'You told your dad everyone thinks he's cool?' she said, very slowly.

'I had no choice, did I? I had to put the cheese in the trap.'

'I know,' said Maddy, 'but I so wish you hadn't done that.'

'Why do you say that?' I demanded.

'Because you've encouraged him. Now he really believes he is down with the kids – and those parents can be the scariest of all.'

'Scary? What are you talking about?'

'You'll see,' said Maddy. 'You'll see.'

Baked Bean Man

CHAPTER SEVEN

Kids with Attitude

Thursday 3 October

5.30 a.m.
Been awake for ages. Far too excited to sleep.
My days as an unknown comedy icon could
be over.

8.00 a.m.
Elliot's just found out I'm going to be on *Kids
with Attitude* tonight. 'You won't win,' he said.
'Your jokes aren't funny enough.'

'Cheers for that,' I said.

'But I know a joke,' he went on. 'A really,
really funny one.'

'What is it then?' I asked.

'If I told you my joke, you'd win for certain.'

'Well, come on then,' I said, interested despite myself.

And Dad, rushing off on his way to work, called out, 'We're a team in this house, so tell Louis your joke, Elliot.'

But Elliot ran upstairs shouting, 'No, I won't, because he steals things out of my bedroom – and he smells funny.'

'Oh, get lost, Little Legs. It's probably a rubbish joke anyway,' I muttered.

But I'd still like to have known what it was.

1.00 p.m.

The number one subject for school mockery is still yours truly. Most people were too busy yelling out, 'I'm looking for my blood!' and asking if my dad wanted to hang out at a party on Saturday to hear my news.

And the few people who did listen said they'd never heard of *Kids with Attitude*, and I was bound to be rubbish anyway. All except Holly, who said she'd definitely be watching, and Julie, who wished me 'tons of luck' between sneezes.

Dad's home early from work, just as he'd promised.

'In honour of this special occasion,' he announced, 'I've even bought a new shirt.'

'Good for you,' said Mum at once.

'I'll put it on now. It's called a fun shirt.'

That worried me instantly. Someone of my dad's age shouldn't be wearing anything linked with fun. But nothing could have prepared me for the total hideousness which was unleashed when Dad returned.

He was wearing the noisiest, most mind-blowingly gross, psychedelic yellow shirt I'd ever seen. It was so disturbing I couldn't stop staring at it. Mum was gazing at it pretty open-mouthed too.

Dad started jumping about, delighted by our responses. 'You thought I'd buy something grey-minded and old-fashioned, didn't you?' He grinned at Mum. 'I've always loved bright shirts – remember?'

'Of course,' said Mum. 'They were like your trademark.'

'I saw it in the shop today,' said Dad, 'and it seemed to call out to me.'

'Scream out, more like,' I murmured, and then I turned to Mum. 'Ask him, Mum . . .'

'Ask him what?' she asked.

'Ask him if he's kept the receipt, because he can never wear that shirt outside this house, can he? Come on, Mum. I saw your face when Dad first galloped in.'

'I was shocked for a second,' she admitted. 'It's so easy to slip into being dull and safe, but now I love it.'

'Not really,' I said.

She smiled. 'In fact, I think it's awesome, and wicked and sick.'

Dad giggled delightedly.

Then Maddy arrived. I hissed at her in the doorway, 'Brought your sunglasses?'

'Why?' she asked.

'You'll need them when you meet the walking headache.'

A few seconds later Dad rushed past us. 'Yo, Maddy, all ready for a sick night?' he called.

97

After he'd gone, Maddy was trying so hard not to say 'I told you so,' the effort nearly choked her.

Then Elliot bounded over to us. 'Hey, where's that amazing joke then?' I asked.

'You'll find out,' said Elliot.

'How will I?' I asked.

But Elliot just laughed.

6.10 p.m.

I've just found out Elliot's joke.

We were being driven to the studio – Maddy and I in the back, Dad sprawled out in the front. Mum had made us some sandwiches to eat in the car, all nicely wrapped in foil. Mine were my favourite – ham and cheese. I took one mouthful and then started coughing so madly the driver had to swerve to the side of the road.

I dived out, unable to speak. All I could do was choke a lot. And finally I dragged it out from my throat – Elliot's joke, or its soggy remains, anyway.

Elliot had written out the joke for me and thought it would be ever so funny if he stuck it between the slices of bread in one of my sandwiches. I gulped down water, while spitting out more bits of Elliot's joke.

I still don't know what Elliot's joke is.

But I've just thought of another one.

'Doctor, Doctor, I've just swallowed a bone.'

'Are you *choking*?'

'*No, I really did.*'

6.45 p.m.

Now we're in the studio waiting room. Dad's wearing a jacket, so partly protecting people's eyes from his shirt. But he's also wearing his trainers with the tongues out and the laces undone and says 'Yo' to everyone who comes in. Unsurprisingly, no one is rushing to sit next to him.

A woman and her daughter did sit next to Maddy, who promptly sneezed twice. Immediately the woman sprang to her feet and demanded, 'Have you got a cold? Because Cora is very sensitive to germs.'

'No, I haven't got a cold, honestly,' said Maddy. The woman went on glaring at her.

'She looks as if she'd like to kill you,' I whispered.

The boy opposite us overheard and grinned. I grinned back.

'Hey, I'm Louis, I tell jokes.'

'I'm Ben,' replied the boy. 'And I don't do anything much.'

'Sounds like a top act to me,' I said.

'I'm part of a double act, and Benny isn't here right now.'

'Where is he then?' I asked.

Ben turned to the man sitting beside him – he was tiny, with a bright red face and looked a bit like a baked bean. 'Where exactly is Benny right now, Dad?' he asked.

'He's resting,' said Baked Bean Man, and that's all he would say.

Then a girl with orange hair and matching glasses arrived.

'Yet another contestant,' murmured Dad.

But then the girl clapped her hands. 'Hi, everyone. I'm Evie, the producer of *Kids with Attitude*.'

'But I really thought she was a contestant!' exclaimed Dad, a bit too loudly. 'Amazing.'

'And it's good to see all fifteen of our contestants here,' she went on.

Fifteen! I groaned inwardly. That's a lot

of contestants to beat. This could be very tough.

'And now,' said Evie, 'I'm going to introduce you to someone I really hope you don't meet later.'

In marched a boy who looked as if he'd escaped from a nursery rhyme. He was wearing some weird kind of uniform, making him look like the head of Toytown or something. He was also holding a truly massive trumpet.

'Now you know,' said Evie, 'that everyone in the audience has a trumpet which they can blow whenever an act is not entertaining them. We call them our mini-trumpeters. But if the audience's trumpets sound too loudly, then our master trumpeter here will appear on stage and he will make this sound. A quick demonstration please, I think.'

The master trumpeter let out a very deep, gloomy sound – the kind of noise an elephant with a secret sorrow might make. 'That noise means you must stop instantly,' said Evie. 'But if the audience allows you to perform for the full three minutes, you will be invited back on stage at the end of the show. Then the audience will vote for their favourite contestant. The winner this week will win a weekend in Paris for him or her and family. And the runner-up will win a weekend in Brighton.

'The winner will then be automatically invited onto our Grand All-Winners Final. And the runner-up has a chance of going on that show too. Now for the all-important running order. I've put all your names in this special bag here. And I'm just going to pull them out as if you were contestants in a raffle. So, let's see who's opening the show. First out is . . .'

Everyone tensed madly, hoping it wouldn't be their name out first. It's always better if you can watch an act or two first before going on. Besides, the person opening the show hardly ever wins. That's a known scientific fact.

And then I heard my name.

'Oh no,' gasped Maddy. My thoughts exactly, but she quickly whispered, 'No, you'll be just fine.' Then Dad touched my shoulder for a moment. And both he and Maddy were smiling so bravely at me, I felt terrible.

'Hope you're not too shocked,' said Evie to me.

'Not at all,' I said. 'I'm just glad this was only a rehearsal. So when are you doing the real draw?' Everyone laughed, and then Evie said, 'Your supporters will be sitting right at the front, cheering you on. If you'd like to say goodbye to them now.'

'I know you'll be brilliant,' said Maddy.

Then Dad stuck out his hand. We had to touch fists with everyone watching. And when he shouted out, 'Safe,' a couple of people giggled. Then I was ushered away by the trumpeter while Evie continued the draw.

A jolly-looking woman bunged some powder on my face and said. 'That's all you need, love, you're handsome enough.' I had a feeling she said that to every single contestant, but still, it was good to hear.

And I truly wasn't that nervous. OK, I had the worst spot. But still, I'd be doing what I loved best in the whole world – telling jokes. Only this time I'd be on television before an audience of – well, I wasn't sure how many people watched *Kids with Attitude*. But it must be thousands, at least.

Then Evie reappeared and led me to the edge of the stage. I took a quick peep around.

It was much bigger than I'd expected — at least four times the size of our school hall. Right at the front I saw Dad and Maddy and other people from the waiting room, including Cora and her mum, who were now sitting as far away as they could from Maddy.

But every other row was filled with people who only looked about thirteen or fourteen. Most of them were blowing their trumpets already, and others were yelling out stuff which I couldn't hear very clearly. But none of it sounded exactly friendly.

Evie saw me sneaking glances at the audience and said, 'They truly are kids with attitude, aren't they?'

Up to now I'd thought the show's title referred to the acts. Now I realized it was actually the audience.

Evie said, 'We wanted to really shake up talent shows which have become so bland and safe. So we decided the key element was to have a very edgy, very hard-to-please young audience. Anyway, we'll be ready to start soon. So you wait here.'

I'm still waiting to go on.

How do I feel? Well, looking at that audience

makes me feel as if I'm about to step into a nest of rattlesnakes. No wonder my legs are distinctly wobbly.

Hey, I think we're about to start at last. I'll be just fine when I'm out on that stage, won't I?

Dad's 'FUN' Shirt

CHAPTER EIGHT

Something Impossible Happens

Thursday 3 October (cont'd)

7.45 p.m.

Only I wasn't fine at all.

It was all the trumpets. Everyone was blowing them before I'd even started. So walking onto the stage with that din going on put me right off.

And instead of coolly strolling onto the stage, I scuttled on like a lost three-year-old, and when I reached out to grab the microphone I skidded. I only just stopped myself from falling flat on my face.

Can you imagine how terrible that would

have been? Me belly-flopping onto the stage.

Shaking more than a bit, I yanked the microphone out of the stand and began telling my first joke. Only I'd never used a microphone before. I thought they just broadcast as soon as you held them. So I was chatting away not realizing no one could hear me. Finally someone yelled, 'Why don't you switch it on?'

'Hey, great idea,' I said, 'you can come again.' And I fumbled about looking for the switch – but I couldn't find it. What was the matter with me? I was acting like a total moron.

Finally Evie sped onto the stage and switched it on in about a millionth of a second and whispered to me, 'We won't start timing you yet,' and shouted at the audience, 'Come on, give him a chance,' as trumpets were blaring out all over the place now.

So I didn't even say *hello*, just started my first joke again.

'What's black and white and eats like a zebra?' But that didn't sound right. In fact it couldn't have been more wrong. I'd given away the punch line already. What was happening to me? 'I mean,' I shouted into the microphone, which I was still holding like an unexploded bomb, 'what's black and white and eats like a horse? *A zebra.*'

Right at the front I could hear someone killing themselves laughing. Well, two people to be precise . . . Maddy and my dad. But no one else was paying me the slightest attention. They were too busy blowing their trumpets. And out of the corner of my eye I could see the master trumpeter. He was getting ready to march onto that stage and declare me out.

So tonight the truly impossible had happened – I'd messed up telling a joke. I've never felt more ashamed of myself.

Any moment now my big chance will be over. Who knows when I'll get another one? To be honest, I didn't deserve another one.

For a second there I nearly gave up, but then I thought of Dad and Maddy killing themselves laughing – at the worst-told joke ever. Talk about loyalty. You could say they inspired me because suddenly I yelled into the microphone a joke I hadn't meant to tell. The one I'd made up after choking on Elliot's joke sandwich.

'Doctor, Doctor, I've swallowed a bone . . .' I kind of gabbled it, but at least I didn't mess it up. It got a laugh too – and not just from Maddy and Dad this time. Trumpets were still blowing away too, but hearing that laughter gave me a shot of much-needed confidence.

Then I just started belting out jokes at the audience, not even pausing for breath between one joke and the next. I was like a one-boy joke machine. The laughter started drowning out the trumpets, while the master trumpeter slunk back into the wings. And soon laughter was reverberating right around the room. I tell you, at that moment I wouldn't have swapped places with a millionaire.

And then that was it – my time was up. The audience gave me a massive cheer. A few were even on their feet. And I was so busy taking bows I didn't see Evie come smiling up behind me. Well, I smacked right into her, didn't I? But the audience just carried on laughing. OK, they probably thought I was more than a bit clumsy and couldn't switch microphones on, but after a very dodgy start they'd decided I was funny too.

Then I joined Maddy and Dad in the front row, where we could watch the other contestants.

'You were brilliant,' hissed Maddy to me.

'Rubbish at the start,' I said.

'It's a bad call, going on first,' said Dad.

'And you so turned it round,' said Maddy. 'At the end it was as if you were just sharing all your best jokes with the audience and really enjoying yourself.'

'I was.'

'And they were a tough audience,' said Dad.

8.25 p.m.

They certainly were.

Act after act got trumpeted out before they'd finished. Two singers had hardly started. Only Cora made it to the end of her act. She was a surprisingly good juggler.

'It looks like it's going to be between you and Cora,' said Maddy.

But then came the last act – Ben and Benny.

Ben shuffled onto the stage with a mouth organ. Already trumpets were starting up. But then he announced, 'Meet Benny,' after which he gave a loud whistle and a grey parrot flew across the stage and onto Ben's shoulder.

Then, while Ben played the mouth organ, Benny sang – or rather squawked alongside him. Benny's screeching made my fillings vibrate and was about as tuneful as someone scraping their nails up and down a wall, but it was oddly brilliant at the same time. The audience let Ben and Benny perform to the end. Then Benny gave a little bow and flew away off stage to huge applause.

After that, the three contestants who hadn't been trumpeted out – Cora, Ben and Benny, and me – appeared on stage again, and Evie told the audience to vote for their favourite.

We'll know the result in about forty-five minutes.

8.30 p.m.
So now there's only Cora, Ben, me and our families in the waiting room. And the tension is just electric. We all want to win so much – even Ben, though he keeps on pretending he doesn't care.

Then I noticed Maddy texting on her mobile. 'Hey, you're not getting me work already, are you?' What an agent.

She looked embarrassed. And so she should. She'd only been texting Edgar. 'Well, he doesn't normally watch television so I wondered what he thought of the show.'

'And what did he think of it?'

Now Maddy looked even more embarrassed. 'He thought the show plumbed new depths of nastiness for a reality show – but he did enjoy most of your act.'

'Most of it!'

'Well, not the very start when you went a little bit wrong,' said Maddy.

'I'd like to see how long Edgar would have lasted out there,' I muttered.

'Edgar just said—' began Maddy.

'Sorry,' I interrupted, 'I fell asleep for a moment there, as this is the most boring conversation ever.'

Then Evie sped into the waiting room. 'The results are in, and it's very close.'

'Tell us then,' I said.

'I'll tell you out on the stage in five minutes,' smiled Evie. 'So not long to wait now.'

We all got up.

'Well, good luck, everyone,' I said. 'And may the best girl, boy or parrot win.'

Maddy got up too. 'You so deserve to win,' she whispered.

'Hadn't you better check with Edgar first,' I replied.

No time to write any more.

Wish me luck.

9.20 p.m.

My heart was beating out of my chest as I waited on stage for the result. First Evie said she'd announce the runner-up. Of course, several years passed before she actually said any more.

And finally she said – *my name*!

So I got the silver medal. And like most silver medallists, I was chuffed but so wished I'd won the gold.

Who did win? Guess. That's right – Ben and Benny the screeching parrot. Of course I congratulated them. And Benny even flew onto my shoulder for a second and gave my ear a little peck.

'But Benny never does that with strangers!' exclaimed Ben. 'He must really like you.' So there you go – I've made a new friend at last. I wonder if he's on Facebook. (I bet he is.)

Later Dad observed, 'They say never act in films with animals – well, never appear in competitions with them either.'

And Maddy said, 'But you were the top solo human.'

As I was leaving, Evie said she'd be sending me details of my all-expenses-paid weekend in Brighton for me and my family. I'd actually forgotten about that. She thinks it will be in two weeks' time.

She also said that she and the executive producer would be personally auditioning all the runners-up on the show and selecting just one for the All-Winners' Final. 'And that is going to be something,' she said, 'because we're holding it at the Royal Albert Hall.'

'So how much do I have to bribe you to pick me?' I asked. 'I've got eighty pence on me now. Will that do as a down payment?'

Evie replied that the audition would be quite demanding but she'd be in contact with me about that soon.

'Meanwhile,' she said, 'congratulations on . . .' She hesitated for a moment.

'On nearly winning,' I cut in, and she laughed.

11.05 p.m.

Back home, and everyone's still awake here –
even Elliot, who is writing me pages and pages
of jokes for my audition. Mum's made us all
a special celebration supper (I'm immensely
tactful, so I didn't point out to Mum how she
very nearly wrecked my chances).

Dad said, 'I hope after your success tonight
you'll still talk to us unfamous mortals and
this won't go to your head.'

'Well,' I said, 'I have now roped off a VIP
area in my bedroom which, of course, only I'm
famous enough to enter.'

Mum and Dad fell about laughing.

11.20 p.m.

Dad drove Maddy home, and as she got out of
the car she whispered to me, 'You're in the big
time now, Louis.'

'Wish I'd won though.'

'But often in talent shows it's the person
who comes second who does the best,' said
Maddy. 'We'll just have to make sure you get
picked at the auditions for the All-Winners'
Final.'

I grinned. 'We sure will.'

We were top friends again now. I didn't mention our little spat over Edgar and neither did Maddy. She did say though, 'Do try and keep your dad indoors as much as possible – especially when he's wearing that shirt.'

11.50 p.m.

Tonight I nearly won a talent show. I did win a holiday.

Best of all, I made an audience laugh.

And I wouldn't swap anything – no, not even scoring the winning penalty at a World Cup Final – for that experience.

I Lost to a parrot

CHAPTER NINE

The Scariest Five Words Ever

Friday 4 October

8.00 a.m.

I woke up feeling surprisingly depressed. Well, it was all over. And I just didn't want my life going back to normal again. So I really appreciated an early morning text:

After your storming act last night it was hours before my pulse calmed down and returned to normal. Keep up the good work, as this is just the start.
　Your agent.

3.15 p.m.
'Who got beaten by a parrot?'
'I wouldn't have voted for you.'
'Your dad's funnier than you.'

That's a quick sample of the comments I attracted at school today. As for my teachers – they just asked me why I hadn't done last night's homework. What is the matter with them? Don't they realize talent shows are our nation's future?

5.10 p.m.
My agent rang – she's arranged for the local paper to interview me and my family at half-past ten tomorrow.

Saturday 5 October

11.35 a.m.
The reporter stayed over an hour and must have chatted to me for all of five minutes. The rest of the time Elliot showed off – which I'd expected. But my parents – especially my dad – kept talking away to the reporter too.

Still, I don't mind sharing my fame.

Monday 7 October

12.30 p.m.

On the way to the shops today a little kid taking a puppy out for a walk rushed up to me saying he'd seen me on *Kids with Attitude* and could he have my autograph. He said, 'This might be worth something if ever you get famous.'

I will never turn away a fan, not even one whose pen leaks over me – and whose puppy left me his autograph all over my shoes.

Thursday 10 October

5.50 p.m.

I'd been wondering why I hadn't heard anything more about my prize for nearly winning *Kids with Attitude*. Well, now I have heard something. Evie called to confirm the date of my all-expenses-paid weekend in Brighton. It starts on October 19th. Next weekend. So, hardly any time to wait really.

Friday 11 October

9.05 a.m.

The local paper is out and my interview is half a page on page five. There are two pictures of me – both with and without my family. These pictures have made me confront a bitter truth. One day I will grow into my ears, but I haven't yet. While my teeth are also too big for me, and leap alarmingly out of my face when I'm smiling – which I am in both of my pictures.

If you're a fan of giant teeth and ears, then I'm your boy. But otherwise, it's just lucky I can tell jokes.

The paper got Mum's age right (forty-four) but gave my dad's as *thirty*-five. It's only a misprint, but I've never seen Dad look more pleased with himself.

Sunday 13 October

3.20 p.m.

At Maddy's house I watched her recording of my act on *Kids with Attitude*. I had my head in my hands at the start. 'Just nerves,' said

Maddy briskly. We analysed how I can make my act funnier next time.

Edgar wasn't there today and Maddy never even mentioned him. I expect even someone as kind as Maddy got incredibly bored with all his poems and showing off. He pretended to be all deep and oracle-like. But that was just a pose. I am very glad Maddy has finally seen through him.

Tuesday 15 October

6.45 p.m.

The sun shone like blazes today and the weather forecasters say it's going to get even hotter by the weekend. Apparently we're in for a bit of an Indian summer with one of the warmest Octobers ever. So, perfect weather to visit Brighton.

More good news. Elliot doesn't want to come with us this weekend. He'd rather go with a friend to Alton Towers. So Mum's arranged for him to stay at this friend's house while we're away. And I was straight on the phone to Maddy saying we had a spare room and would she like to come to Brighton. She said 'Yes' almost before I'd finished asking the question.

Thursday 17 October

7.20 p.m.

Dad's bought himself another shirt for Brighton.

You should see it, dear diary. It's a green, psychedelic one, which in the solar system of revolting things is right up there with the yellow one. It's also at least one size too small, so you can see all his rolls of fat, even if you don't want to, which I don't.

Worst of all, Mum was with him this time and apparently fully conscious while he made this demented choice. Yet she made no attempt to stop him.

'He always was a flashy dresser,' she said fondly.

Yes, back when fire was being discovered, maybe.

Of course neither of my parents has given me a second thought. They have no idea of all the mental anguish I'll suffer having to walk beside Dad dressed like that.

Besides, if anyone should be parading about in wild, wacky shirts now, it's me. I'm allowed. But my parents have had their turn. Only now they want another go. It's just not fair.

9.00 p.m.

To ensure I don't sleep tonight, Dad's just announced that when he was with Mum he bought some other stuff for the weekend.

My flesh is creeping already.

Friday 18 October

5.50 p.m.

I have bought Maddy and me some huge sunglasses. If we wear these and keep several paces behind my parents at all times, we should be spared total embarrassment.

Saturday 19 October

9.00 a.m.

The day started so well, with the sun peeping through the curtains and the birds doing their stuff. This trip to Brighton was going to be epic. And not even my dad's appalling taste could spoil it.

Then I spotted Maddy walking briskly towards my house. It was so great she was coming too. I opened the door. 'You're just in time,' I said.

'For what?' she asked.

'For me to open the door for you.' I grinned.

She smiled. 'You're in a good mood.'

My good mood lasted for two more seconds. That's when I saw who was trailing behind her. Edgar. His hair was even messier than usual and he was blinking furiously, like a mole that had just been dragged out of its hole and into the daylight.

Maddy was going to have to do something about him. He was becoming a big nuisance. And what was he doing here now?

Edgar, with a big flourish, put down Maddy's bag and called out to me, 'I just want you to know I have no difficulty at all about this weekend.'

What on earth was he talking about? I hadn't a clue. Probably best to humour the loon. 'That's great news,' I said.

'Brighton wouldn't be my choice,' he went on. 'It's too commercial. I like somewhere quieter and more secluded where I can be right away from the howling masses and really think.'

'Lucky you're not coming too then,' I snapped.

And then Edgar leaned forward and gave Maddy a little kiss on her right cheek. After which they hugged. I nearly fell over with shock – and horror.

When he'd sloped off I said to Maddy, 'He just kissed you.'

'I did notice.' Then she added, 'Well, he is my boyfriend.'

I nearly fell over again.

'Since when?' I asked.

'Since he asked me out four days ago.'

'Why didn't you tell me before?'

'I tried to, but you've been so busy,' she said more than a bit feebly. 'I thought you might have guessed,' she went on.

'No,' I said softly. 'I really didn't see that coming at all.'

'But you are happy for us?' persisted Maddy.

Happy she's going out with the biggest idiot I know? What could I say? Nothing. So I just sort of shrugged. And it was hard even showing that much enthusiasm.

'It won't affect me being your agent,' she continued.

'I should hope not,' I said. Did I mean to say that, and in such a gruff, miserable voice? Probably not. But I was too dazed to know what I was saying.

Then Maddy let out a gasp. She'd just spotted my dad striding down the stairs. Not only was he wearing that green psychedelic shirt which looked even more hideous in daylight, but also some stripy blue, red and white shorts.

'Yo, Maddy, all ready to chill by the sea?' he called.

'Oh yes, can't wait,' replied Maddy, smiling bravely at him.

'So let's hope we have a sick time,' said Dad. 'Laters.'

After he'd gone Maddy said gently, 'That can't be at all easy for you.'

But actually I was still reeling from her news.

10.10 a.m.

We're on our way to Brighton now, with Dad and Mum in the front of the car and being so enthusiastic about absolutely everything they're wearing me out.

While in the back Maddy's had a text from Edgar *already*.

'That's so wrong,' I said. 'He should let you just enjoy yourself. Not bombard you with texts every five minutes. That's actually very inconsiderate.' Then I noticed how upset Maddy looked. He hadn't dumped her already, had he?

'So, what did he say?' I asked. 'I suppose he wrote it all in rhyming couplets.'

'No,' began Maddy, and then whispered a few words so faintly I couldn't hear her properly. But it was something about Edgar thinking it was cold.

'No way is it cold today,' I began, 'not even in his world.'

Maddy gave a very small, unamused laugh. 'No, Edgar texted that the universe feels so cold and lonely without me.'

'He's determined to try and ruin this trip, isn't he?' I muttered. 'And I bet he didn't make that up – he's copied it out of a book somewhere.'

'Oh no, he hasn't,' said Maddy firmly. 'I hope Edgar will let you read his poems some day and you'll see just how dedicated he is. He's got so much untapped potential, you know.'

Maddy used to say I had untapped potential. But now it's all Edgar, Edgar, Edgar. And even when he wasn't texting, it was still as if Edgar was sitting in the car between Maddy and me, killing the atmosphere stone-dead.

Before today Maddy was the one person I could really talk to. Yet now I can't, because all at once she seems years older than me. Maddy's ageing fast, while my parents – now singing along far too loudly to a One Direction song – are getting younger every second. And getting the words wrong . . .

Why can't everyone just stay the same? Like me. I've no intention of ever changing. I'll always be Louis the Laugh.

12.45 p.m.
We're in Brighton now and have just checked into the Waverley Hotel, which is quite

small – just sixteen rooms – but right on the seafront.

A bored-looking boy behind the desk gazed blearily at us when we arrived. Then Dad showed him the pass from *Kids with Attitude*. Without another word the boy got up and walked into this small office just off the reception area and hissed, 'This week's runner-up is here.'

Then he stared at me for a moment. 'You lost to a parrot, didn't you?'

'I'll have that put on my passport soon.'

The boy added, 'The manageress will be out shortly.' And seconds later a small, bustling woman with a perm the colour of tomato ketchup rushed over to us. She looked like the friendliest dinner lady you've ever seen.

'Well, a huge welcome to you all,' she cried. 'I'm so delighted to be your prize.' She made it sound as if she personally was my prize, which made Maddy and me giggle a lot. Then my parents started giggling too. And soon everyone was laughing hilariously for no particular reason.

The manageress burbled on about the lovely weather we'd brought with us and how we'd picked a special weekend to be here, as they were having a party at the hotel tonight to mark The Waverley's tenth birthday.

There was also going to be a big raffle with some wonderful prizes. All the guests had complimentary raffle tickets. She handed Mum ours and then said to me, 'I'd be so honoured if you, as this week's visiting celebrity, would pick out the winning tickets in the raffle this evening. Around half-past nine?'

Afterwards Maddy said, 'You're the visiting celebrity. Isn't that magical?'

I couldn't deny it really was. Then I said, 'Still, I expect Michael McIntyre and Jack Whitehall get asked to pick out raffle tickets all the time.'

'But now they have a rival raffle-ticket-picker,' said Maddy. 'You.'

5.00 p.m.
This is the highlight of the day so far because –
- We're all sitting by the hotel pool.
- We've just been given three tons of free sandwiches and cake.

- We've not had any new texts from Edgar for at least an hour.
- I just did this impression of the way Dad keeps wiggling his sunglasses, which made Maddy explode with laughter. And it's as if she's the Maddy I know again.
- Both Mum and Dad are fast asleep. Earlier they went pelting round Brighton (followed at a considerable distance by Maddy and me in our dark glasses), but now they are flat out. I have also slipped a towel over Dad, totally hiding his shirt and shorts. So no one would guess he is currently insane.

7.55 p.m.

On the way to the hotel party, Maddy and I called for Mum and Dad.

Dad opened the door. He'd gelled his hair up into a kind of quiff (just as he'd done in that ancient snapshot of himself). He'd changed his shirt too – he was now wearing the yellow psychedelic one, as well as jeans, boots and a silk scarf. He also had a silver hoop in one ear. He looked like a geriatric pirate.

'So, what do you think then?' he asked Maddy.

'You look so . . .' began Maddy, blinking wildly.

'So horrible,' I muttered.

'So colourful,' said Maddy at last.

Dad grinned. 'I was always known as a bit of a striking dresser. I don't think I've lost my magic touch, do you?'

What do you say to such a seriously deluded parent? What *can* you say?

Then Mum strode in from the bedroom wearing tight leather trousers and a grey sparkly top.

Dad stepped back. 'The sands of time keep moving, but they've stopped around you.' Then he said to Mum, 'You don't know me, but I've seen you on the bus a few times and wondered if you'd like to go to a party tonight?'

'Well, I might,' said Mum in this weird, girlie voice.

'So how about if I call for you about eight,' began Dad. After which he and Mum fell about laughing.

Then Dad said to Maddy and me, 'The first time I ever saw your mother we were on a bus and she was looking so incredibly beautiful. Every night I'd sit on the same bus and just stare at this gorgeous apparition.' Mum started acting all mock embarrassed then. 'Finally I plucked up my courage and asked her to a party, never dreaming she'd say yes.'

'I nearly didn't,' said Mum. 'But I'd noticed him on the bus too and thought he seemed quite nice-looking.'

They were off now on their own private time machine, as Dad went on, 'Of course, at the party I wanted a kiss, but every time there was a slow dance I lost my nerve, until there was just one slow dance left and everyone was going onto the floor . . .'

'And then the Vikings attacked,' I said. 'Honestly, it's great you can still remember back to those ancient times. You had to do your homework with a chisel and a piece of stone, didn't you? But we're going to be late for the party if we don't go now.'

As we were leaving, Maddy said to me, 'Your parents are weird – but fun weird.'

'You don't have to live with them.'

'No,' she continued, 'but I thought what your mum and dad were saying was kind of cute.'

'And kind of nauseating,' I said.

8.15 p.m.

We let my parents go into the party first. 'Then we can stand right at the opposite end of the hall to them,' I said.

Maddy and I hovered outside the party lounge. Then two girls stopped right in front of me. 'You were on the talent show where the parrot won,' said the taller girl to me. 'But you should have won,' she added.

'We would have voted for you,' said the other girl.

I smiled modestly and chatted away to my public. They wanted to know all about *Kids with Attitude*. Maddy must have got bored (or even, I add hopefully – a bit jealous) because she drifted into the lounge.

When the girls finally left I saw Maddy coming back out of the lounge, only she was walking very oddly now – sort of staggering as if she'd just had a huge shock.

'What's wrong?' I asked.

'I peeped in at the party,' she said slowly. 'There's some music on and' – she took a deep breath before uttering what just might be the five scariest words ever – 'your parents have started dancing.'

I swallowed hard. 'I bet they're rubbish.'

Maddy moved closer to me. 'They give new meaning to the word dire.'

I swallowed hard again.

'But you don't have to see them,' said Maddy. 'Save yourself – go somewhere else.'

I was very tempted until I remembered something. 'But I've been specially asked to present the raffle prizes at half-past nine. Of course I could send my apologies and say I've just come down with the plague.'

'Yes, I'll tell them you're very sorry but you're too ill,' said Maddy eagerly.

But being a future comedy icon does have its responsibilities. And not backing out of presenting the raffle prizes was definitely one of them. So I said, 'No, I'm going in.'

Sometimes my bravery amazes me.

8.40 p.m.

I deal in comedy, not horror, so I shan't dwell long on what I saw at the party.

We were greeted at the door by a smiling boy handing out paper hats which Maddy and I promptly lost. (I refuse to wear a paper hat, even on Christmas Day.) But most of the other people there had shoved them on. And the manageress was striding about with a gold crown perched on top of her perm. 'Enjoying yourselves?' she boomed at this couple, and then, 'That's wonderful!' before she'd even heard the reply. There were waiters speeding around with trays of food and drink, and music from the olden days was pounding out.

People of all ages were there, but the majority looked about my parents' age. A few of the men were dressed up in dinner jackets and vile-looking bow ties, while the women had on these low, floating dresses. Some of the guests had settled on a long row of chairs looking just as if they were waiting for a train. Others were in little clusters, nodding in time to the music. And all were gazing with a kind of horrified fascination at what was happening right in the centre of the room.

My parents were still dancing.

They weren't doing that kind of half-hearted dancing oldies do at weddings either, where they just stroll about on the floor. No, Dad was really rolling his head about as well as making these very bizarre strutting movements. He looked like a turkey who was in a right strop. While Mum just kept vigorously shaking herself and generally acting as if someone had put masses of itching powder down her knickers.

I'll spare you any more details. I'll just say no one else was dancing – too scared, probably.

I tried to catch Mum's eye. I thought seeing her son might just remind her that how she behaves reflects on me.

But Mum only cried, 'Ah, here they are at last. Ask Maddy to dance, Louis. You'd like a dance, wouldn't you, love?'

'Well, not right now,' began Maddy.

Then Dad waved at me. 'We're really kicking it, aren't we? Rup and Maria should see us now.'

I edged closer to them. I tried to be tactful. 'Could you both just take it down a bit, please?'

Dad roared with laughter. 'Louis is telling us off,' he cried. 'He doesn't approve of us having fun.'

Mum giggled. 'Tonight, Louis, rebellion is in the air – and we're going to really enjoy ourselves.'

I so wished my parents would stop twittering on all the time about enjoying themselves. It was unnatural.

But I couldn't make them see sense. So I went back to Maddy, sighing heavily. 'They won't listen to me.'

'That's because they're locked in a world of their own,' murmured Maddy.

Sometimes Maddy's wisdom amazes me.

10.05 p.m.

The raffle was very late starting and all that time my parents never left the dance floor. I kept hoping Dad's knee would pack up again. But no such luck.

The two girls I'd chatted to earlier wandered in, gazed at my parents and chorused, 'Er, gross – or what?' Then they spotted me, and something in my manner (or maybe just that my face was as red as a beetroot) must have alerted them to my shocking parentage.

'That's your mum and dad,' they cried.

'I'm adopted, I hope,' I replied.

They laughed.

'They'll be fine when they've had their medication,' I went on.

They laughed again.

'And if you think that is embarrassing, you should hear what my dad did at the end of the school disco . . .'

I was still relating this grim tale (and both the girls were falling about laughing) when the raffle finally started. I was called to the front and described as one of the stars of *Kids with Attitude*. Then I started picking out the winning tickets. And what a lot of winners there were. One being . . . Dad. He bounded over, took his prize – a huge box of chocolates – and said to me, 'Your face looks familiar.'

I wish yours didn't, I thought.

I slipped in some jokes as I made the raffle draws and when I'd finished I received what Maddy called afterwards 'a storm of applause'. Then the music was on again and my parents promptly returned to the dance floor.

'This is the best fun we've had . . . for years, Louis,' shouted a wild-eyed Mum at me.

I didn't say anything. I just gave her a very disapproving glare.

'They are now completely out of control,' I said to Maddy. And I couldn't bear to watch any more, so we went for a walk on the beach. I said, 'All I want are dull parents who dress quite drably and are happy in their oldness. That's not too much to ask, is it, Maddy?'

'No, it really isn't,' she agreed.

'And mine used to be exactly like that.'

'I remember.'

'So, how can I change them back, Maddy?'

'What we need is a game plan,' said Maddy. 'I'll do my best to think one up.'

'And soon, Maddy.'

'Don't worry, I know how urgent it is,' she said. 'But maybe . . .'

'Maybe what?'

'Maybe the worst is over now. They've let their hair down and re-lived their youth so they'll be happy returning to being normal parents again.'

Sunday 20 October

8.30 p.m.

Back home and my parents do seem calmer, quieter and older tonight. Could Maddy be right? Is the very worst over?

Monday 21 October

7.50 p.m.

Maddy is totally and completely wrong. My parents' behaviour has just plummeted to new depths.

You won't believe what they've done now.

CHAPTER TEN

De-friending Your Parents

Monday 21 October

7.50 p.m. (cont'd)

Tonight Mum announced, 'We've joined the Facebook party.'

'You've what!' I spluttered.

'Your dad and I have started Facebook pages,' said Mum.

'We thought it was about time we did,' added Dad.

Then, bursting with pride, they each displayed their handiwork. They were, without doubt, the worst Facebook pages I'd ever seen.

For a start, Mum had put herself down as male. Most of the pictures were upside down ('Perhaps you could show us how to turn them the right way up. We got a bit muddled about that,' said Mum). There was also a toe-curling message from the goldfish ('Thank you very much for feeding me every day. I love that new food') and a picture – upside down, of course – of me on my potty.

I'd have been worried if I hadn't noticed how many friends they both had – just the one. Each other.

'Yeah, I'll help you,' I said. 'But actually, you don't want to clutter up your page with snaps of me. You want lots of jolly pics of you two weeding or cleaning the car or something.'

Smiling coyly, Mum then leaned forward and said, 'We also wanted to ask you if we could "friend" you on Facebook. Is that the correct term?'

I was too horror-struck to reply at first. I just stood there, grinding a few teeth.

'Look at his face – you've obviously said it wrong,' said Dad.

'But can we?' she persisted.

I just couldn't believe they were asking me

such a thing. My Facebook is for me and my mates – and no one else. I certainly couldn't have my parents sniffing about on it. It was absolutely nothing to do with them. This was a total invasion of my privacy.

They must have seen my stunned expression, because Dad said jokingly, 'Oh yes, we'll know exactly what you've been up to now.'

'But you haven't got anything to hide, have you?' smiled Mum.

Of course I have. What person of my age hasn't?

'But don't worry, we're the new generation of parents,' said Dad. 'The cool ones.'

'And you can tell us anything at all,' said Mum. 'We won't be shocked.'

All right, how about this? You are the last people in the entire world I'd want roaming about on my Facebook page. And this isn't because I don't like you, as I do, most of the time. But BECAUSE YOU'RE MY PARENTS, and I'm a completely different person around my mates than I am with you.

Instead I said, in as friendly a voice as I could manage, 'Yeah, of course you can friend me on Facebook.' *They'll soon get bored of this*, I thought. I hoped so, with all my heart.

Tuesday 22 October

6.45 p.m.

For an unhilarious laugh my parents have now started leaving silly messages on my Facebook wall. They put one up first thing today asking if I'd remembered to wash behind my ears today. 'You could grow turnips behind Louis's ears' was their side-splitting final line.

Maddy was appalled when she saw their messages. 'I'm thinking so hard of a game plan,' she said.

Wednesday 23 October

4.00 p.m.

I'd just arrived at school when Julie, after giving an ear-splitting cough said, 'Your mum and dad really freaked me out last night.'

I was stunned. 'But how? Where did you see them?'

'I didn't see them – they sent me a Facebook message.'

'Now I am so confused,' I said, 'that I may pass out.'

Then Julie showed me the message:

Hi, Julie – Do you like *The Simpsons* – we do. In fact, it's just about our favourite show. Have you got an episode you really like – we'd love to know? Marlon and Jessica.

'And I thought,' said Julie, 'who on earth are Marlon and Jessica? I'd never heard of them in my life. But here they were sending me this weird message. It really worried me until I found out other people were getting Facebook messages from Marlon and Jessica too.'

'They've messaged other people?' I said hoarsely.

'Oh yeah, loads of people on your Facebook had got messages from Marlon and Jessica asking what their favourite films and albums were and—'

'No, no, no,' I groaned.

'I was just so relieved when I found out they were your parents. I thought it might be some mad people.'

'No, my parents are not exactly mad – they're just having a bit of a flip-out right now and meddling in stuff which is nothing to do with them.'

'I haven't replied to their message,' said Julie.

'No, don't encourage them in any way,' I said firmly. 'Thanks for taking it so well. And tell everyone else – I will sort this out.'

5.15 p.m.

Maddy has also received one of my parents' cheery messages, asking about her favourite foods.

Then Theo told me that he and some of my other mates from my old school had also been contacted by Marlon and Jessica.

'Just tell your parents very firmly,' said Maddy, 'that sending messages to your friends is not something they should ever do again.'

7.00 p.m.

I asked my parents for a word.

'Got a problem, Louis?' asked Dad.

'Yes, you two,' I wanted to answer. But instead I said, as casually as I could, 'I hear you've been sending Facebook messages to my friends.'

'That's right,' smiled Dad. 'Just to introduce ourselves and find out a bit about everybody.'

'And be friendly,' added Mum.

'But the thing is, parents don't go round sending messages to their children's mates. It's just not something they ever do.'

'Until now,' said Mum.

'So we're the rule-breakers,' said Dad. He looked dead chuffed about this.

'Actually, when you sent those messages . . .' I paused. 'Well, you and Mum came across as a tiny bit weird.'

'But weird can be good,' said Dad at once. 'Weird can be a trail-blazer.' Then he added, 'They're just not used to cool parents.'

But there's *no such thing* as a cool parent. Parents are either dull and boring, which is what you want – or an embarrassment. There are no other options.

I just can't get Mum and Dad to see this.

I stared at them in mounting frustration. 'The thing is, everyone at school has asked if you'd stop sending them messages, as it just confused them. And I'm asking you as well.'

148

Too angry to say anything else, I stormed into the kitchen. Seconds later, Dad was there too.

'They were just very short, very friendly messages.' He sounded indignant.

'I know, I saw one.'

'We thought it would be good for us to know what young people are thinking. And they might enjoy hearing our views too, especially as we're cool parents.'

'Well, I'm afraid they don't,' I snapped.

'Not any of them?' asked Dad.

'No.'

'I never realized young people today were so ageist, so quick to pigeon-hole people.'

Now he sounded hurt. And I felt bad, yet I was also annoyed with Dad for making me feel bad, because he was in the wrong – not me.

8.00 p.m.

Maddy tried to cheer me up by reminding me it's my birthday tomorrow.

'Do you know, I'd *almost* forgotten,' I joked. 'Ha. We'd be living in dark times if I could forget something as vitally important as my birthday.'

'*I* hadn't forgotten,' said Maddy lightly.

'So what have you got me then?' I asked.

But she wouldn't tell me, said it was a surprise.

Thursday 24 October

8.30 a.m.

My birthday. And already my parents have left a message on my wall. They wished me a happy birthday and urged me 'to groove on and have fun with your homies. With love from your cool fam.'

I tell you, one more message like that – just one more – and I'm de-friending them both for ever.

Mum trying to be cool

Yo

CHAPTER ELEVEN

The Worst Shock Yet

Thursday 24 October (cont'd)

9.15 a.m.

Some fairly decent presents, including an Xbox from Mum and Dad and a massive bar of chocolate from Elliot, which he'd only nibbled a little bit. I also picked up some extra cash for not having a birthday party. I'm mighty relieved I accepted that bribe now. Well, can you imagine how my parents would have behaved? They'd have wanted to join in all the dancing and friend everyone on Facebook.

Instead, Mum and Dad are taking Elliot, Maddy and me out for a lavish meal somewhere. So I shall spend most of tonight just filling my face with food. Brilliant!

7.20 p.m.

The evening started so well, but then . . .

Good bit first. Maddy gave me a cracking present – a first edition of *The Mating Season*, a Jeeves book by my comic hero, P. G. Wodehouse. It was so old and valuable I told her I'd put gloves on every time I read it and clean my teeth before I dared breathe anywhere near it.

'It must have cost you a fortune,' I said.

Maddy didn't argue.

'I bet you had to take out a mortgage to buy this – still, I'm worth it.' Then I leaned forward and gave her a kiss – well, more like a peck really. But when you get really top-class presents, you've got to do something to show your appreciation, haven't you?

And for a moment there I wished with all my heart that Maddy was going out with me, not Edgar. It was all over in a flash. And it was obviously caused by the shock of such an ace gift. Maddy looked shocked and a bit stunned too.

I said, 'So that shows you how much I loved your present.'

'It sure does.'

Then Mum sped in from the hairdresser's. She really did look better before she'd gone. Her hair was all frizzy and sticking out now. She looked as if she'd had five electric shocks all at once.

Elliot stared at her, fascinated.

'In honour of your birthday,' said Mum.

'You really shouldn't have bothered,' I muttered.

'I'm so sorry about that,' I said to Maddy after Mum had left.

'No, it's fine.'

'You're getting used to shocks in my house,' I said, 'but I'll try and make sure we sit Mum at the darkest table . . .'

I stopped talking.

I stopped breathing for several seconds. I'm sure Maddy did too.

For coming down the stairs was my dad, and he was wearing . . .

I'm sorry, but I must stop for a moment.

The full horror of what I'm about to tell you has just hit me all over again.

CHAPTER TWELVE

I Turn into Batman

Thursday 24 October (cont'd)

7.25 p.m.

Sorry about that, but I still cannot think of what Dad wore without getting goose pimples. But I'm calmer now and ready to tell you everything.

Dad pranced down the stairs wearing that hideously yellow fun(!) shirt and a pair of tight, red leather trousers.

But it was what he was wearing on his head that caused my blood to freeze.

He was wearing a baseball cap with a gold

logo and he was wearing it the wrong way round.

There are many things in life you never wish to see. But let me tell you, there's no horror like seeing your dad in a baseball cap the wrong way round.

It doesn't say: *I'm still hip, I'm still young.* It can only ever say one thing: *I'm totally and completely desperate.*

In fact, Dad might as well have put a sign on his back saying that.

Maddy whispered, 'Probably best if you look away for a few seconds. Try and get used to it in stages.'

I hissed back, 'I'm *never* getting used to it. Dad has totally crossed the line now.' Then I said in as friendly a voice as I could manage, 'That baseball cap's new, isn't it?'

'Just got it today,' said Dad.

'And it's great—' I began.

'Thank you,' interrupted Dad.

'For wearing around the house,' I went on, 'and when you're doing a spot of hoovering or window cleaning. I'm sure it's got tons of uses for indoors. It's just not right for wearing out of doors.'

'Unless you're doing some gardening,' added Maddy helpfully.

'I can see how it's a bit of a shock,' said Dad, 'seeing your once-stuffy dad wearing a baseball cap – round the wrong way. Only that's how they're all wearing it now, isn't it?'

'Everyone who is a teenager, yeah,' I said.

'But fashion is for everyone these days,' said Mum, smiling now. 'There are no silly age barriers any more.' So, she's been thoroughly brain-washed as well.

'We're all free to express ourselves today,' went on Dad breezily. 'We'll be ready to leave in about ten minutes, all right?'

Then he and Mum trooped off to the kitchen. I had this sick, helpless feeling at the pit of my stomach and I stared wildly at Maddy. 'I can't let Dad go out like that.'

'You really can't,' said Maddy.

'No, you can't,' agreed Elliot. 'I've got my reputation to consider, you know.'

'So what can I do?' I said.

'Hide it in the garden,' suggested Elliot.

'No, take too long. Better to just burn it or lock Dad up for the rest of the year? Come on

Maddy, what should I do? Help me. And we haven't got much time,' I added.

Maddy thought for a moment. 'OK . . .' she said slowly. 'Now your dad's totally lost the plot.'

'I know that,' I said impatiently.

'So as he's gone a bit mad, you're going to have to be especially brave and strong. Be Batman to his Joker.'

I liked the sound of that.

'But,' went on Maddy, 'even Batman needed Robin to help him out and rescue him sometimes, didn't he?'

'Yeah, he did,' I agreed. 'But I'm not sure where you're going with this now.'

'Am I Robin?' asked Elliot eagerly.

'Not this time,' said Maddy. 'It has to be someone who can back you both up. Somebody who your dad will have to listen to . . .'

'But who?' I began.

And then Elliot shouted out, 'Nan and Grandad.'

I gaped at him. 'For the first time in your life, Little Legs, you've nearly said something intelligent. Nan and Grandad will hate seeing Dad in a baseball cap round the wrong way as much as us. And they haven't seen Dad since his birthday, so they'll be shocked by his whole outfit.'

'And they'll go on and on about it too,' said Elliot, 'because they go on and on about everything.'

'Well, he'll have to listen to his parents,' said Maddy. 'So there we are, we've found your Robin – or Robins.'

'I kind of like you comparing me to Batman,' I said, dialling my grandparents' number. 'A comedian by day and a superhero at night. Yeah, I'll go with that.'

Then I was through to Grandad. And after I'd thanked them both for their book tokens I said, 'Actually, don't panic but this is a kind of emergency phone call. Could you and Nan come round right away?'

'Why, whatever's happened?' asked Grandad. 'Is everything all right?'

'Well, it is and it isn't, if you know what I mean.'

'Not even remotely,' said Grandad.

'I really think it's best if you come round – and see for yourself,' I said, then added, 'And would you let Mum and Dad think you've just popped round because it's my birthday, OK?'

'We'll be there in about fifteen minutes,' said Grandad. 'And don't ever end a sentence with OK.'

I've never waited for my grandparents more eagerly.

Dad thinks he's SO cool but he's NOT

CHAPTER THIRTEEN

Dad Is Sent to His Room

Thursday 24 October (cont'd)

9.05 p.m.

What a night!

I tell you, it's all been kicking off here.

It all started when Nan and Grandad finally turned up. Mum and Dad had been ready to leave for ages, while Maddy, Elliot and I desperately played for time. I opened the door before my grandparents had time to ring the bell.

'Hey, what a surprise!' I said.

'Yes, isn't it,' said Grandad.

'But we were in the area,' said Nan, 'and

thought we'd pop in and wish you many happy returns.' She patted Elliot rather absently on the head. But all the time she was talking she and Grandad were staring around anxiously.

Then Grandad spotted Maddy. 'Ah now, who is this young lady?'

'This is Maddy,' I explained. 'She's looking after my career.'

'But how splendid,' said Grandad, acting a bit suave with Maddy. 'I'm very pleased to meet you, my dear.'

Nan smiled briefly at Maddy too and then asked, 'So what's so urgent, Louis?'

'It's Dad,' hissed Elliot. 'And what he's got on his head.'

'On his head!' echoed Nan. 'What do you—' She stopped in mid-sentence. Dad had bounded out of the kitchen. Nan reeled and Grandad did some very vigorous deep breathing exercises.

'Who's your friend?' Grandad muttered to me at last.

'No one I know,' I muttered back.

But Dad seemed totally unaware of the impact he was making, and just smiled cheerily round at Nan and Grandad. 'Hey, have you dropped by to wish Louis a happy birthday? That's so kind of you.'

'It certainly is,' said Mum, now standing beside him.

Nan did another double take at the sight of Mum's new hairstyle. 'What have they done to themselves?' she whispered to Grandad. It was one of those whispers you can hear five miles away.

But Mum just said breezily to Nan, 'It's called retro-style,' and then added, 'It's so lovely to see you both but unfortunately we're just on our way out.'

'We shan't keep you long,' said Grandad. 'We've just got one question for you.' He turned to Dad. 'What on earth have you plonked on your head – and why?'

'That's two questions,' said Elliot.

'You came all the way here to ask that?' said Mum.

'I'll tell you the truth,' said Grandad. 'We received an SOS from Louis. You might say the young and the old are joining forces on this one,' he added. 'I don't even like baseball caps on teenagers, but on someone of your age . . .' Grandad did some more deep breathing exercises.

Then Nan, who'd been peering at Dad through eyes that were as thin as needles, continued briskly, 'So just take that ridiculous thing off your head, Marlon, and go upstairs and put your real clothes back on. Then Louis can enjoy his birthday meal – and we can go home.'

Dad suddenly burst out laughing. 'I can't believe it. You're actually sending me to my room. You haven't done that in thirty years.'

Mum seemed far less amused. 'He's a grown man and is free to wear whatever he wants.'

'Well, I'm very surprised at you letting him go out like that,' Nan snapped back at Mum. 'I'd never let my husband go out dressed like—'

'Like he belonged in the world's oldest boy band,' I interrupted.

'You do look so weird, Dad,' said Elliot.

'And actually,' chipped in Maddy, 'being cool is about looking as if you're not trying, while you look like you're trying ever so hard . . . Sorry.'

'And I do believe it sends the wrong message to the neighbours,' said Nan.

Suddenly Dad raised a hand at all of us. 'Right, I think we're done now,' he said, quietly but authoritatively. We all thought he was going to say something else. I think Dad thought he was as well, as he actually opened his mouth a couple of times. But he must have changed his mind, because instead he stomped upstairs, just the way a very frustrated and angry teenager might. Moments later we heard his bedroom door slam shut.

'Dad really *has* gone to his room,' shouted Elliot excitedly. And it was kind of exciting, but shocking too. What was Dad going to do now? I looked at Maddy. She shrugged.

Mum, clearly not at all happy, said, 'Will you just excuse me for a moment?' and sped upstairs as well.

'Now Mum's gone to her room too,' said Elliot. 'This is brilliant. When will you let them out, Nan?'

Nan gave a grim little smile and then whispered to Grandad, 'I hope he doesn't start sulking now. When he was a boy he could sulk up in his bedroom for hours. Remember?'

Grandad nodded and then added, 'I think you went a bit too far sending him to his room.'

'I didn't actually send him to his room,' said Nan. 'I just told him to get changed, so don't turn on me.'

'I'm not,' said Grandad. 'I'm merely pointing out—'

'You never backed me up in disciplining him when he was a boy. Nothing's changed,' snapped Nan.

The atmosphere was getting tenser by the second here, while upstairs . . .

I whispered to Maddy. 'What if he doesn't come down again tonight?'

She giggled and I did too. I felt as if anything could happen now.

What did happen is that a couple of minutes later Dad came back down the stairs. He was without his baseball cap and instead wearing his oldest, drabbest suit – it reeked of mothballs – while leaning heavily on a walking stick, which I'd never seen him use before. 'I hope I'm dressed appropriately for your birthday now, Louis.'

Mum was smirking beside him, obviously

thinking this was such a clever little joke against Nan, Grandad and me. But actually I'd be happy if Dad always dressed like that. Parents can never dress too stuffily.

'And if you don't have any other concerns,' said Mum to Nan and Grandad in an icily polite voice, 'we'd better leave for our meal now, since we're very late as it is.'

Grandad whispered to me as he and Nan walked out, 'We're in the doghouse now.'

'Not with me,' I whispered back. 'You played a blinder and the baseball cap is history.'

The birthday meal itself was very awkward. Everyone was pretending so hard to be cheerful. But now and again Mum would stop smiling and then she'd just look dead cross. She was furious I'd sent for Nan and Grandad. I felt terrible, but good at the same time. Yes, I'd been tough, but I'd helped Dad see the error of his ways too.

I really thought that.

Then, at the end of my birthday meal, I received a shock. Dad hadn't referred to the baseball cap until we were about to leave, and then he said to Maddy and me, 'I know how you and my parents have a boring, staid image of me. My fun-loving rebellious side can be a bit of a shock. I completely see that. So I'll wait a little while before I unleash my baseball cap again.'

Wait a little while . . . ?

Hadn't Dad learned anything tonight? And didn't he have any concern for me? The shock of seeing him in a baseball cap round the wrong way was not something I could just wipe from my mind.

I know it'll take time.

But the thought of it happening again – of maybe meeting Dad outside when he's stalking about in it in full view of everyone I know – well, it would probably take me years to get over an experience like that.

'Never have I needed your game plan more urgently,' I said to Maddy.

'Don't worry, I am working on it,' she said. 'And I should have an idea very soon.'

She really is an agent in a million.

Edgar & Maddy. URGH!

CHAPTER FOURTEEN

Edgar to the Rescue

Friday 25 October

3.00 p.m.

Horrific news. We've got another history test next month. Our teacher's obviously got this freaky addiction to tests, as well as seven chins.

And why is the eighteenth century so boring and complicated? And why have I still not got a clue what's going on? Actually, I think history lessons are deliberately designed to annoy me – and make me feel stupid.

I'll have to get out of the next test somehow.

Or maybe I'll be discovered before then and rescued from my very dark future.

Only bright note, it's half term next week.

5.45 p.m.

Evie's called with the date of the auditions for all the runner-ups to be the one in the All-Winners show – it's in two weeks' time, on Wednesday November 6th. She also had a bit of a bombshell for me.

She said, 'We're going to ask you not to tell jokes as you did last time. Instead, we want you to take a topic – any at all – and be very funny about that, for three minutes. But without telling a single joke.'

'What we'd really like, Louis,' she went on, 'is for you to have an attitude about something and explore that in your performance. And also tell us a little bit about the real Louis – let us into your life.'

'But no actual jokes,' I said.

'Not one,' she said firmly.

7.15 p.m.

Just told Maddy. 'Don't worry,' she said, 'I'm on to that too.'

170

Saturday 26 October

6.00 p.m.

Guess what? Maddy's called and reckons she has solved both my problems at once – namely, my parents and what I'm going to talk about on *Kids with Attitude*. This sounded excellent until she added, 'Or rather, Edgar has.'

'You discussed my private problems with him?'

'I told you before – he is my boyfriend.'

Normally I really, really like Maddy – but there are moments when I could go right off her – and hearing her blurt that out again was definitely one of them. I *know* Edgar is her boyfriend. But there's no need for her to keep mentioning it, is there? That's news she should keep to herself.

'I think you'll be very impressed with Edgar's ideas,' she went on proudly. 'So, do you want to come round now?'

'Will Edgar be there?' I asked.

'Of course he will,' she said.

I was so tempted not to go round.

But these are desperate times.

6.30 p.m.

There are some people who can annoy you after saying just one word. Edgar is definitely one of those.

'Hello,' he said at the door, sounding so smug and pleased with himself.

Just one word and I want to tear off his head. Of course I didn't. I even managed to grin at him (I really have got untapped acting talent).

Then Edgar said, 'Thanks for coming round,' just as if this was his house, not Maddy's.

Then we went up to Maddy's bedroom. She and I both sat down while Edgar shambled about, flipping his curly hair around and muttering, 'I've solved both your problems.'

'I'll be the judge of that,' I said.

'Do you want to listen to what I've got to say?' asked Edgar.

'I'm sure it'll be the highlight of my life,' I said.

Edgar sighed, and so, I regret to tell you, did Maddy. I've never felt further away from her than I did right then.

'Maddy told me,' said Edgar, 'that you regaled some girls at Brighton with tales of your parents' recent behaviour. Do you remember?'

'Of course I remember,' I said.

'Maddy also told me that the girls were highly amused, so it seems obvious really. You give your comedy talk about your parents' appalling behaviour. You couldn't have a better subject than that.'

'And you've got loads of material,' cut in Maddy, 'with them dancing and going on Facebook and—'

'Yeah, yeah,' I interrupted, 'I see that.'

'You should also – and very, very soon,' said Edgar, 'let your parents hear this talk, telling them you want their opinion of it—'

'But really,' interrupted Maddy excitedly, 'you'll be telling your parents exactly how they're totally embarrassing you – and themselves.'

'Only you're using the healing balm of laughter,' said Edgar, 'so they won't be offended.'

'No, they'll be laughing too hard for that,' said Maddy, 'but they'll also be thinking hard, and by the time you've finished they'll see the error of their ways. Isn't it a perfect plan?'

'It has possibilities,' I conceded very reluctantly. Actually, I thought it was a top plan, but I wasn't going to say that.

'And can you write the talk tonight or tomorrow?' asked Edgar.

'Yeah, why?'

'Because your parents need to hear it urgently. I wouldn't normally be so forceful,' he went on, 'but when I heard about your father wearing a baseball cap the wrong way round' – he swallowed so hard all his curly hair shuddered – 'well, we really want to prevent the next stage.'

'Do you know what the next stage is?' I asked.

'I do,' said Edgar, 'because it happened to an acquaintance of mine at my last school. His dad, like yours, was desperate to be "down with the kids". Behaviour, I must say, I find quite inexplicable. But anyway, he had already done most of the things your dad has put you through. Then, one day after lessons had finished, this boy was starting to go home when he saw someone breezing towards him. It was his dad romping down the road with a skateboard under his arm.'

Now my spine was well and truly chilled. 'In full view of everyone he was holding a skateboard?' I quavered.

'I believe someone even took an incriminating photograph.'

I shivered.

'But I believe and fervently hope,' said Edgar, now peering right at me beneath his hair, 'we're still in time to prevent your dad ever doing that.' He seemed genuinely concerned, and shockingly I was about to say something vaguely friendly to him when Maddy's dad called up the stairs, 'It's seven o'clock.'

'Got your dad doing time checks now, have you?' I grinned.

But both Maddy and Edgar looked suddenly awkward. Maddy was even turning red. 'No, my dad's just reminding me of the time,' she said, 'because Edgar and I are going out on a date.'

Well, that was absolutely nothing to do with me. What my agent did in her spare time was her business.

I knew this, but I was also so unsettled I started gibbering, 'Hey, you two going on a date? That's amazing.'

'Why amazing?' asked Edgar at once.

'Well, I don't mean amazing exactly...' What was I talking about? Even I hadn't a clue. I just knew I was suddenly incapable of conversing normally. 'So are you going anywhere particular, or just out for a long walk through the leaves?' I asked.

'To the cinema?' said Maddy.

'Hey, fantastic,' I said, with such forced enthusiasm I cringed inside. I was becoming nearly as embarrassing as my dad. 'I'm sure you'll have a superb time, watching the film and eating popcorn. Be sure and eat loads of popcorn, and then if the film is rubbish you can always throw popcorn at the screen.'

'Actually,' said Edgar, 'we're going to a film club – and they're not terribly keen on patrons consuming popcorn. It can be very distracting.'

'But what if the film is rubbish?' I asked.

'I've seen it before,' said Edgar. 'It's a fine German film, *The Edukators*, about modern-day Robin Hoods ... do you know it at all?'

I shook my head miserably and decided it was definitely time to leave.

Maddy called after me, 'Be sure and write your speech.' I felt as if she were setting me homework.

I walked home slowly and sadly. It didn't matter that both of my problems might well have been solved. My head still felt very heavy. It just wasn't right. Maddy shouldn't be going to a cinema where you can't even eat popcorn. She should be going to quite a different cinema, and with an entirely different person too.

7.45 p.m.

Started my speech for the audition.

Here are the first lines:

'This is a special guide about how to cope with the most embarrassing parents of all – the ones who think they're cool and wicked.'

Good opening lines, I think.

9.50 p.m.

I have re-written my whole speech six times. I've so much to say on the subject of embarrassing parents, it's hard to know what to leave out.

Sunday 27 October

4.30 p.m.

I've just rung Maddy and read aloud some bits from my talk. She nearly had hysterics, she was laughing so much. 'That is great stuff,' she said.

Maddy didn't mention her date with Edgar last night, so neither did I. I'd hate her to think I was being nosy. And I'd hate it even more if she told me she'd had a great time.

6.30 p.m.

I'm ready to perform my act to my parents. I'm going to do it tomorrow. And Maddy said she'd be there too as back-up.

To my surprise Dad said he didn't have to go to work tomorrow. He said he's taking a few days' holiday. It must be great to have your holidays whenever you feel like them.

Still, he'll be in an especially relaxed mood tomorrow night then – and able while he's laughing to see the error of his ways.

Then he and Mum can slip back to being old and past it again.

That's all I ask of them.

CHAPTER FIFTEEN

Weirder and Weirder

Monday 28 October

4.30 p.m.

It's half term (hooray and hooray again), so I've had plenty of time to practise my act.

Bit of an odd atmosphere at home though. Nothing I can really put my finger on, but a lot of whispering in the kitchen between Mum and Dad. I usually assume all whispering is about me because – well, it usually is. But I'm not in any particular trouble at the moment, am I?

6.15 p.m.

Here's what I hope will happen tonight.

My mum and dad will listen to my act and laugh so much they'll have tears in their eyes. While they are wiping their eyes they'll say happily, 'We get it, we've been totally embarrassing, but we'll start acting our age now. And thanks so much for showing us the error of our ways in such a hilarious way.'

9.50 p.m.

Real life never goes the way you want, does it?

Here's what actually happened tonight. Maddy, Mum and Dad were all in the sitting room and I was about to start when I noticed Mum and Dad were holding hands. Now, I've nothing against them doing this, but I'd just prefer they do it when they're not in the same room as me.

And it slightly put me off.

'Not nervous, are you?' asked Mum.

'Don't worry, we'll be a good audience,' said Dad, now hanging onto Mum's arm as if they were about to take off into space.

'Well, here it is,' I said. 'My special guide

about how to cope with the most embarrassing parents of all – the ones who think
they're cool and wicked.'

Maddy was smiling already. My parents
both looked a bit stunned.

'So,' I went on, 'you've got to look out for
the warning signs. Firstly, when your parents
start asking you about the current slang – or
"the word on the street", as they might call it.
Listen very carefully to what I'm telling you
now. Never tell them anything. Not one single
word – unless you want your parents turning
up at your school gates yelling, "Yo, where's
my blood?" (I did a great impression of Dad
here.) Yes, that really can happen. I know.

'Next we come to one of the most horrifying
sights you will ever have to see – parents
dancing. This is always distressing, but one
day you might see your parents like this.'

Then I launched into a wild impersonation
of Mum and Dad dancing, which had Maddy
in absolute hysterics. In fact, she nearly fell
off her chair she was laughing so much.

My parents were much more restrained.
Mum was hardly moving at all – it was as if
she'd been turned to stone – while Dad just

sat massaging his chin. They didn't exactly fall about when I talked about parents trying to find you on Facebook or Dad wearing a baseball cap the wrong way either.

Then I pressed on with the other part of my talk – the proper procedure for dealing with cool parents.

'Now you know the signs,' I said, 'what should you do? Firstly, act fast. The moment your parents do stupid dancing or babble, "Yo, where are my homies?" say firmly, "No, this isn't meant for you, you've had your day. My world – not yours." Repeat that phrase at them over and over. "My world – not yours." And tell them that even if they rock up in leather trousers and the latest trainers, carrying a skateboard' – yes, I'd used Edgar's material; it was too funny not to include – 'it's no good. They can't cheat their way back in. They can never be cool again. All they can ever be now is an OAT. That's an old-age teenager. And who really wants to be that?

'I'd like to end by dedicating this performance to my parents – without whom my act wouldn't have been possible – or necessary.'

I ended to deafening applause from Maddy

and not quite so deafening applause from my parents. Worse, my parents hadn't laughed once.

'Thank you for that thoroughly deserved applause. So what did you think?'

'That was just genius,' said Maddy.

'I can see why you might think that.' I grinned. 'But what do the rest of my audience think?'

'It was certainly well performed,' piped up Dad at last.

'Mmm,' said Mum.

'We weren't expecting this though,' said Dad.

'No, we weren't,' agreed Mum.

'A tiny bit of it was inspired by your illustrious selves,' I said.

'We puzzled that out,' said Mum.

'But it's not just about you two,' I went on, 'is it, Maddy?'

'Oh no,' said Maddy at once. 'It's about lots and lots of parents. Parents all over the world, actually.'

'Oh, really,' said Mum softly.

'I didn't hear you two laugh very much,' I said.

Dad gave a wry smile. 'Too painful.' He jumped up. 'In fact, I've been squirming all the way through it. Anyway, if I promise never to dance again, I hope I'm excused to have my bath now.' Mum looked a bit startled by Dad's sudden exit and I heard him murmur to her, 'No, I'm fine,' before striding to the door, and then smiling very cheerily at Maddy and me. 'Thanks for a sick time. And that's the very last time I'll ever say that. I think you'll do very well with that act, Louis.'

Dad was saying all these positive things. And he seemed to have learned something too, so why did I still feel so uneasy? Perhaps it was the awkward silence after he'd gone.

Then Mum stood up too. I thought she was going to leave as well. But instead she stood there, swaying about as if she'd just been hit by a bullet and any second was about to tumble to the floor.

'Maybe after your talk,' she said suddenly, 'parents will be given a right to reply.'

'Ha, ha,' I said, as if Mum had made a joke. (I don't think she had.)

Maddy grinned away too.

'Really, what you're saying,' went on Mum,

'is that parents should feed, clothe and pay for you, but whenever we're not doing any of these things, then we must just shuffle off into the background, preferably in the darkest, drabbest clothes possible.'

I couldn't have put it any better myself. Say what you like about my parents, they're quick learners.

'Exactly right, Mum,' I said.

'And you know,' continued Mum, still swaying madly, 'you really should issue a guide book about all the words parents are not allowed to use. Let me just check with you now – *wicked*, for instance.'

'Wicked is one you should definitely stay away from,' I said. 'Although I really like the way you said it – just the right speed.'

'And what about *cool*?' asked Mum.

'You might get away with that one,' I said, 'if you say it really fast, as you did then.'

'And of course you can still say, it's a cool day,' added Maddy helpfully, 'if it *is* a cool day.'

Mum nodded and went on. 'But words like *yo* and *my blood*, and *sick* in its non-vomiting form . . .'

'Avoid at all costs,' I said. 'I can write you out a full list of words you must never use, if you like.'

'How kind,' murmured Mum. She'd stopped swaying and was standing right in front of me now. 'And when your friends come round, am I actually allowed to speak to them at all? I'm still a little confused on this point.'

'Oh yeah, you can chat with them when they arrive,' I said, keen to be generous. 'Or when you first see them. Just remember to keep the conversation very short and not ask too many questions.'

'But don't appear as if you don't care,' added Maddy.

'And it's all right to wait on your friends with food and drink,' said Mum, 'provided when I come in with the tray I don't start speaking again.'

'It's probably safer,' I agreed.

'Some parents just knock on the door and leave the tray outside,' added Maddy.

'What a truly excellent suggestion,' said Mum, shooting to the door, 'which I'll put into action now. I'm assuming you'd both like some more tea and sandwiches.'

'Yes please.'

'Well, I'll sort that out for you. I will knock on the door when the tray is ready for you to pick up – and I shan't say another word. See how quickly I'm learning the correct way for parents to behave.' And with that she was gone.

I turned to Maddy. 'At first Mum seemed like she was being so reasonable.'

'No, she was being sarcastic,' said Maddy. 'My mum does that too sometimes.'

'Really, she's sensationally angry, isn't she?'

'Seething,' agreed Maddy.

'As for Dad,' I said, 'he was so upset he had to leave, didn't he?'

'Well, it was mainly about him,' said Maddy.

I shook my head gloomily. 'So much for Edgar's healing balm of laughter.'

'You can't blame Edgar,' Maddy said at once. I just knew she'd defend him.

'I wasn't blaming him,' I said, although I was really. '*And* I used his example of the skateboard. I'm just saying his idea hasn't helped the situation.'

'I don't agree,' said Maddy. 'Maybe it's a good thing your parents are so worked up.'

'I don't follow.'

'Well, it shows they were really listening to what you said. I'll tell you something else. I bet you've stopped your dad parading around the streets with a skateboard.'

A shudder ran right through me. 'If Dad ever did that I'd have to get a new identity.'

'And if your dad ever did that I'm sure the government would let you do just that,' said Maddy, 'but you needn't worry about that now.'

'And you still think I should do tonight's act about parents on *Kids with Attitude*?'

'But of course you must do it,' insisted Maddy. 'It's the best thing you've ever done. And your parents will be fine about it once they've got over the shock.'

But would they?

They'd been weird all day – and now they were acting even weirder.

Sometimes parents are nothing but a big worry.

Dad's
'FUN'
Shirt

CHAPTER SIXTEEN

A Shocking Discovery

Tuesday 29 October

8.00 p.m.

I'm always hoping that one day school will die out.

Everyone – teachers included – will just get fed up with it. Of course, I'm fed up with it already. So the very last thing I want on my few precious days away from doing hard labour is to talk about school.

But that's what I've just had to do and . . . well, you just wait.

This evening I was doing some unpaid manual work – loading the dishwasher –

when Mum and Dad sort of both whooshed beside me. All day they'd been OK but a bit distant. I couldn't blame them, I suppose. Now they seemed distinctly friendlier.

'Hey, dude,' said Dad.

'We can still call you *dude*?' asked Mum.

'Why not,' I said. I was feeling generous.

'Be patient with us, we'll get it right in the end,' said Mum, with a definite edge of sarcasm. 'Anyway, we've just been looking at the syllabus of your new school.'

'You really know how to enjoy yourselves, don't you?' I murmured.

'And we've just realized something,' continued Mum. 'At your old school you hadn't yet reached the eighteenth century in history.'

'Oh, time moved very slowly there,' I said vaguely.

'But it can't be easy for you,' said Dad, 'being so far behind the rest of the class, as at your new school we see they've been studying the eighteenth century for the past term.'

'When you're as clever as what I am, such concerns are mere trifles,' I said, very eager to change the subject.

'You certainly did very well in your history test,' said Mum. 'Did Maddy help you at all?'

'Mum, what a question! Go and wash your mouth out this instant, I'm deeply insulted,' I said, ever so cleverly not actually answering that one.

'I really think she might have,' Mum persisted. 'Anyway, we're going to help you, by arranging for you to have a tutor for history and . . .'

I stared at Mum with undisguised horror. 'But why – I haven't done anything especially wrong lately.'

'It's not a punishment, it's to help you catch up and to make life better for you,' said Mum. 'We knew you'd be pleased,' she added. That sarky tone had returned to her voice. And I did even wonder if this was payback for last night.

But then I remembered all the hissing I'd heard in the kitchen yesterday. I'd guessed it was about me. And so it was. That probably also explains those odd, shifty looks Dad had given me lately. He knew what a terrible thing was about to be inflicted on me.

Wednesday 30 October

2.00 p.m.

And now for some quite surprising – and very surprising – news.

The quite surprising news is that my parents seemed to have stopped leaving messages on my Facebook page.

As for the very surprising news: you remember Dad's fun shirts? How could you forget them, dear diary? Well, I've just seen them both – in the bin. Dad has obviously dumped them.

I did have a scramble about to see if he'd got rid of the baseball cap as well. I couldn't find it. But still, this is real progress. I'm delighted – but a bit stunned too by the speed of it all.

4.30 p.m.

Mum took Elliot to a party this afternoon. Meanwhile Dad was in his office, the hut in the garden. He'd spent the day there having a big clear-out. (Holidays are totally wasted on adults, aren't they?) Anyway, I thought I'd just very tactfully congratulate him on throwing out the fun shirts – and see if I could talk him out of that threatened tutor as well.

But in the end I never said a word to him. I just caught a glimpse of him through the window. He didn't see me. He was too lost in gloom. He was hunched on his swivel chair, looking totally miserable. But why on earth was he looking like that, and on his holidays too? Then I realized why.

He was missing his fun shirts.

They were his very last chance of being young again. So when he threw them away he was throwing away a dream too. And who had smashed his dream? Me.

I did it with the best intentions – to stop him embarrassing himself, and me. But now Dad looked about nine million years old.

I'D MADE MY DAD LOOK NINE MILLION YEARS OLD.

That is not good. In fact, it's terrible.

I was too shocked to know what to say to Dad after seeing him like that.

Later he was back in the house acting all cheerful.

But I know what I saw.

Dad bought those fun shirts because they seemed to be calling out to him. Well, now they've started shrieking at me. They never let up. So I have just been out to the bin and rescued them, shuddering all the time.

The thought of Dad wearing them makes me shudder even more. But I was too honest with him before. And adults just can't take that. I should have gently eased Dad off those shirts. My cure was too extreme. So now I shall tell him he can still wear the fun shirts, just preferably when I'm not with him.

I have just slipped the shirts into the bottom of his wardrobe. I'm sure he'd like to be reunited with them in private. And if he asks me about the shirts later, I'll just very casually say that, yes, I put them there as I thought he'd thrown them away by mistake. And they are really starting to grow on me – and are nowhere near as bad as I first thought.

I truly have a noble character.

Thursday 31 October

10.30 a.m.

It's Halloween. After Christmas, the happiest day of the year.

At breakfast Dad, Elliot and Mum all jumped out at me in the kitchen, wearing horror masks. I pretended to be scared. Elliot loved that. 'You looked really frightened,' he kept saying.

'So, trick or treating tonight?' I asked Dad.

Every year he and I have done that. Then last year, for the first time, Elliot joined us. He's got a lot to learn is all I'll say about that.

Dad said, 'That's right, Elliot's excited already. I expect you're off out with your buds?'

What buds?

There's still my mates from my old school. But I know Theo's got flu – it's racing round his school. And anyway, last year Theo just went off trick or treating with his dad.

Actually, trick or treating is still OK to still do with your parents. Well, you'd all have masks on for a start. Also, it'd be dark so no one could see you very clearly anyway.

I tried to explain this, but Mum and Dad were too busy leaping about helping Elliot make some spooky decorations for tonight.

Every single year I've gone trick or treating with Dad. But this year he just assumed I'd be too old or too embarrassed without even bothering to check with me first.

That's sloppy parenting, if you ask me.

4.00 p.m.

Unexpected visitors – Nan and Grandad. They pretended they just happened to be in the area. But Grandad hissed at me when I opened the door to them, 'We're here on a peace mission.'

'And there's the boy who started all the trouble,' said Nan to me, not unkindly. Then she asked in one of her piercing whispers, 'And what's your dad wearing today?'

'Now come on, it's none of our business and so we don't care what he's—' began Grandad. Then he stopped as he saw Dad.

I did wonder if Dad might have slipped on one of his fun shirts. He must have found them by now. But he was probably saving them up. Instead, he looked a bit scruffy actually, in an ancient jumper and cords. No baseball cap either. Nan and Grandad instantly relaxed.

Later, when they were leaving and after Grandad had given Elliot and me five pounds each for Halloween, Nan said, 'I found some more photos of your dad when he was young, so make sure you take a good look at them.' She was staring right at me as she said this.

Why on earth would I want to see them?

7.35 p.m.

Halloween is just teeming with dark, dangerous monsters now, and I should be one of them.

I usually wear this mask with bulging eyes and huge, sharp teeth.

But tonight, that mask – my mask – is lying all neglected and unwanted on the sitting-room floor, while Dad and Elliot left about half an hour ago. Dad was laughing and joking all the time, nothing like the nine-million-year-old man I'd spied yesterday. As they were leaving, I saw Dad rest a protective hand on Elliot's shoulder – just as he used to do for me.

Of course, I'm far, far too old for Dad to do

that now. But suddenly it's as if Halloween is only about Elliot. I've been totally discarded. And Dad hasn't even mentioned my great sacrifice – giving him back those revolting fun shirts.

7.45 p.m.

I've just rung Maddy and so wish I hadn't.

I thought we could meet up. But before I was able to say anything she announced, 'Edgar's here.'

'Now that is scary,' I said. 'Edgar's the only guy who doesn't have to bother wearing a mask tonight. In fact, he's more terrifying without one. That's just a joke, by the way. Do give him my worst.'

Maddy didn't laugh or have a go at me. In fact, I've had livelier conversations with myself.

'So, are you both just off somewhere?'

'Mmm,' she said vaguely.

She wasn't even the tiniest bit friendly. And I sensed she wanted me to ring off really fast. So I gabbled, 'Well, I'll say *bonsoir, mi amigo* – you never realized I could speak so many languages, did you? And maybe I'll catch you again before my brain dissolves away. See you.'

That was, without doubt, the dullest, the most humiliating, the least everything you can think of chat I've ever had with Maddy.

She obviously doesn't want to know me when her boyfriend Edgar's there. I could be very hurt by her attitude. I'll just have to lighten the mood by looking through my joke collection.

8.30 p.m.

For once none of my jokes have made me feel any better. So instead I've just sent Maddy a text:

I'm extremely sorry to have disturbed you when Edgar was round your house. I'll try not to do it again. Thanks for the good times. Louis

9.20 p.m.

The trick or treaters are back. As usual, Mum has decorated the sitting room with fake cobwebs and glow-in-the-dark window stickers, and stuck a massive pumpkin in the window. There's even a skeleton reclining on the couch. He pops up every Halloween and is practically one of the family now.

Elliot raced about very over-excited (I'm sure I was never that annoying), and after expressing surprise that I wasn't out somewhere, Mum and Dad invited me to tuck into the Halloween food too.

I still felt like an outsider, until Elliot was finally packed off to bed and Dad said, 'Got something to show you over in the hut, Louis.' Dad wouldn't tell me what it was and was acting more than a bit mysteriously. Was it something to do with the fun shirts?

But instead, laid out on the table in the hut, were a few more photos of Dad in ancient times. Why on earth did Nan and Dad think I'd be so interested? I hastily scanned them. And then I stopped. So Nan had slipped in a snapshot of me. It was what you might call an extreme close-up – just showing my face.

'I don't remember Nan taking this of me . . .' I began.

Dad didn't answer, just fell about laughing.

I picked up the photo and let out a whistle

of amazement. Now I could see it wasn't a picture of me at all. It was of Dad when he must have been about my age. But when I first saw it – well, the resemblance was just uncanny. It was like looking at a twin.

'Dad,' I spluttered, 'what are you doing looking exactly like me? This must stop. Never do it again. Still, one bit of good news, your ears in this picture are as supersonically huge as mine. But they're not now. So that's one thing I've got to look forward to – shrinking ears.'

Dad gave me what I can only call a sly smile and said, 'That grinning, crazy guy in the photos you mistook for yourself – he's still somewhere inside here, you know,' and he tapped his head.

'Say aaah, and I'll find him for you.' I grinned. 'And there's not even a search fee.'

Dad looked as if he was about to say something else, but then Mum called down the garden that Elliot was saying he was too scared to go to sleep now.

'What an amateur,' I said. 'You never had that problem with me at Halloween.'

After Dad left I took one last look at that

photograph of 'me'. Then I was about to leave when I must have knocked against the side of the table as all these papers fell to the ground. I hastily picked them up, glancing at them very idly. I never expected them to be at all interesting but they were. They were all addressed to Dad and said things like: 'Thank you for your application. We don't have any new vacancies at the moment but will certainly keep you on file.' Others were more personal, inviting Dad in for a chat.

But it was obvious what they meant – Dad was looking for a new job. Why on earth was he doing that? He had a perfectly good job, didn't he?

Then I thought of Dad's sudden holiday. The odd atmosphere there'd been in the house all week. And the hours and hours Dad had spent in this hut. It hadn't felt as if Dad was on holiday – because he wasn't.

And when I'd seen Dad looking totally miserable yesterday he hadn't been mourning his fun shirts at all. He was just feeling really bad about being out of work. How many hours had he sat in the hut all alone, his face dark with worry about the future? I suppose Mum knows. She must do. That's probably why she has been extra-nice to him lately.

Suddenly I heard Dad pounding back. I very hastily put the letters back. I knew I wasn't meant to see them.

Dad stuck his head round the door. 'Think we might need reinforcements. Elliot's got himself all worked up, so a few of your jokes are definitely what's needed.'

'Yeah, sure,' I said, feeling oddly awkward with Dad now.

11.00 p.m.

I still can't believe Dad's out of work. Rup had only been at this house a short time ago. And he and Dad seemed to get on so well. What could have changed? Anyway, why hadn't Dad just told me he'd lost his job? Too ashamed? Too proud, maybe?

Of course, I could confront him. 'Hey, Dad, I was having a bit of a nose around the hut when I spied some letters. Bit of a shocker about you losing your job . . .'

No – much, much better if Dad tells me himself.

And he'll have to come clean soon, won't he?

CHAPTER SEVENTEEN

Maddy Tells All

Saturday 2 November

7.25 a.m.

Dear diary, I don't often wake up and jump straight out of bed. Well, never, in fact, until today, when I've just been struck by a thought.

Recently I've glimpsed Dad looking exactly like the world's gloomiest man. And I'm pretty certain he's lost his job. So what am I going to do on Wednesday? Only humiliate him again. For my performance is all about my parents making total fools of themselves.

And it was bad enough for them having

to watch it in the sitting room. They weren't exactly convulsed with merriment then, were they?

But if I get through on Wednesday (a big if, I know), then I'll have to repeat the talk on television. And millions of people will be laughing their socks off at my unemployed dad.

Wouldn't it be better to do a completely different act? It would certainly be kinder.

I've still got time.

8.00 p.m.

Well, it's taken me most of the day – but I think I've done it.

I've now got a brand-new subject – teachers.

Tons of funny stories and jokes – and no humiliation for Mum and Dad. Perfect.

Sunday 3 November

11.00 a.m.

I've called Maddy. Well, she is still my agent. I wasn't very friendly, but then neither was she. I just announced, 'I've changed my act.'

'Why?' she demanded.

'Well, I've improved it – so, do you want to hear it?'

'Of course,' she said, almost snappily.

'So how about hearing it now?'

'Fine,' she said, and then rang off without another word.

12.30 p.m.

When I arrived at Maddy's house I'd never felt more ill at ease. It was all because of Edgar, of course. Any second he was going to spring out at me, babbling about how brilliant he was – and then start kissing Maddy again.

I nearly asked Maddy where he was. But I begrudged him the oxygen. Maddy's family were all milling about so we went up to her bedroom.

'Been to any good firework displays?' I asked, just making conversation.

She shook her head. 'No, have you?'

'No.' Then I decided I'd made enough conversation and announced, 'I've re-written the entire act.'

Maddy gasped loudly. 'But it was brilliant before.'

'Ah, but brilliant's not good enough for me – as you will see.'

I launched into my new act. Last time, Maddy had fallen about laughing. This time – well, I've seen the Halloween skeleton look more amused. When I finished I kind of bleated, 'So what did you think then?'

'Just awful,' said Maddy. 'Terrible.'

'Don't hold back now. I only worked on it all day yesterday.'

'But you put jokes back in again,' she said.

'So you did notice.'

'You've gone backwards. Your act about your parents is fresh and sharp and true. This is just like a load of not very funny jokes about teachers. There's no way you'll be picked for the All-Winners Final on that.'

'In your opinion,' I said.

'In everyone's opinion,' said Maddy. 'This is the biggest chance you've ever had and you're just throwing it all away.' She got up. 'As your agent I'm instructing you to tear this up and go back to your other performance about parents.'

I looked at her. 'Actually, I can't.'

'Why?'

'I think my dad's lost his job. He hasn't told me, but I found out accidentally. So if I get through I'll be making fun of him on TV in front of millions.'

Maddy didn't say anything for a moment. 'But you getting through to the final would really cheer him up, wouldn't it? Plus it could take away one of his problems.'

'How do you figure that out?' I said.

'Well, when you become a top comedian you'll give him some money, won't you?'

'Of course, as much as he wants,' I said at once.

'So there you are,' she said. 'But you losing your chance – your biggest ever chance – won't help him or you.' Maddy went on, 'At least ask your parents if they'd mind.'

'Yeah, I could do that, I suppose. And I will. Thanks.'

Maddy smiled faintly.

'I'll go now then,' I said. 'Thanks for your time.'

I was at the door when she cried, 'Don't go.' I whirled round.

'Last night when you called, I'm sorry if I sounded a bit . . . abrupt.'

'No problemo – you were with Edgar and didn't want to be disturbed,' I said through clenched teeth. 'I totally understand.'

Maddy stared down at the floor. 'Actually, when you called, Edgar was dumping me.'

'What!'

'He just came round and announced that with regret he was dumping me.'

'He said "with regret" he was dumping you. Even when he's dumping someone he's annoying. Still, it could have been worse. He could have written you a poem as well. And then what happened?'

'He wished me good fortune in the future – and left.' Maddy was still looking intently at the carpet.

'It must have been a massive shock.'

'It was.' Maddy's voice wobbled a bit. 'I've never had a boyfriend before and I did think it might have lasted a bit longer.'

'And I rang when he was making his little speech?'

'The exact moment.'

'You should have rung me back after he'd gone.'

'I wanted you to concentrate on your

performance. I didn't want you to be distracted by my news.'

'Distracted,' I echoed. 'I am your friend as well.'

And actually, that news would have improved my day considerably, although I'd much rather it was Maddy who'd done the dumping.

I walked right over to Maddy then, and gave her hand a squeeze. She looked up and squeezed my hand back. 'Edgar will soon come crawling round on his belly,' I said, 'begging you to take the miserable specimen – which is him – back.'

'No, he won't.'

'You sound very certain.'

'I am,' she said softly. She looked as if she was expecting me to pipe up with something else. I was rather hoping I'd say something else too. In fact, I was boiling with the effort of thinking.

I knew exactly what I wanted to say.

'Maddy, I really like you and it would make me so happy if you'd go out with me now, as all the time you were with Edgar I was just aching inside. So Edgar did one good thing anyway: he's made me see you're the only girl for me.'

But I didn't say any of that, because I knew this wasn't the right moment. Not straight after Maddy had just been dumped. And anyway, that sort of stuff is extremely hard for any boy to say, let alone one with massive ears.

But being dumped must be really horrible, even by someone as loathsome as Edgar. And I so wanted to say something to cheer Maddy up, to help her. Especially as she's helped me so many times.

So finally I said, 'Well, look after yourself.'

Wow. Amazing, I know. People will be studying my wise words for centuries. *'Well, look after yourself!'*

And after those highly stirring words I left.

5.20 p.m.

I've just spoken to my Mum and Dad. I said if they didn't want me to do my act about parents on *Kids with Attitude*, that was no problem at all. They looked really surprised.

'But of course you must do it,' said Mum.

'Really?' I said.

'Yes, if we had to listen to it, why should other parents escape? Let them suffer as well.' Mum said this quite sternly, but there was a twinkle in her eye.

Then I looked at Dad. 'I'm cool about it too,' he said at once. 'I am allowed to say cool when we're alone, aren't I?'

'All right, all right.' I grinned.

'Actually,' said Mum, 'your act helped us remember things about being your age. Like how important it is not to stand out – or to be different.'

'Oh no, Mum,' I said. 'It's totally fine for me. I just don't want you two standing out and being different.'

For some reason Mum and Dad found this true fact very funny, and Mum was still laughing as she left to answer the door. Then Dad said to me, 'By the way, did you put some shirts I'd thrown out back in my cupboard?'

'Yeah, that was me. I thought you might be missing them.'

'You did, huh?' Dad grinned slowly. 'I've really been a bit of a try-hard lately, haven't I?'

I couldn't argue with that but I said, 'Oh, don't worry about it, Dad.'

Then he went on. 'You know what's really the problem with parents, don't you?'

'Go on, tell me,' I said.

'We're all younger inside our heads than anyone gives us credit for. But the moment you try and prove that, you're totally sunk. That's why I shall be returning, unmourned, those trying-ever-so-hard shirts to the bin. But I shall be keeping my baseball cap and trainers for now . . .'

My eyes opened wide.

'Just to remind myself of the cautionary tale they tell – but they will soon, I'm sure, find their way to you.'

'Hey, cheers, Dad.'

I wasn't sure if I was thanking him for not embarrassing me tonight, or for the probable new trainers coming my way as soon as my feet caught up with my ears. But I felt Dad was really opening up to me. And I liked that. That's why I then asked, 'Are you on holiday again next week, Dad?' giving him the perfect opportunity to come clean.

But he just said, 'Yeah, that's right, lucky

old me.' He stopped smiling when he said it though.

But he managed to glue a big smile on later. Elliot would never have guessed there was anything wrong as we all stood around the bonfire at the local sports club, watching the fireworks and guzzling jacket potatoes. Halloween felt a long time ago as we all hung out together. And yes, it was *wicked*.

CHAPTER EIGHTEEN

Day of the Audition

Monday 4 November

5.00 p.m.

Out of all the people I never expected to see round my house – put Edgar right at the top of the list.

But shortly after I'd got back from school – there he was.

We faced each other in the doorway.

'I shan't come in,' he said.

'You certainly won't,' I snapped.

He gulped. 'So are you all right? Having fun?'

I gaped at him. 'Why on earth are you

asking me that?' I demanded.

'Just trying to make conversation by talking to you in your own language.'

'Well, I wouldn't bother. I suppose you want to talk about Maddy.'

'Yes, I do,' he admitted.

'You're very sorry you dumped her – and want me to put a good word in for you. You've got a nerve.' I was furious now.

Edgar stepped back. 'Up to now all my good friends have been imaginary. They disappoint you far less than real people, I find. But then I met Maddy and she hasn't disappointed me at all.'

'So why did you dump her then?'

'Because every time I was with her I could see I was merely an interloper. There's only one boy she's really interested in, and regretfully it's not me. Instead, it's someone of far meaner intelligence.'

Before I could respond to this Mum appeared and stared curiously at Edgar. 'Invite your friend in, then,' she said to me.

'It's all right, Mum, he can't stay,' I said.

'No, I can't stay,' repeated Edgar, 'but thank you for your extremely kind invitation.'

Mum gave him another curious look and disappeared.

Edgar went on, 'You're frightened that if you ask Maddy out she'll reject you.' He looked me up and down for a moment. 'And I can see exactly why you might think that. But you have to take a chance. I'm telling you this for her sake, not yours. That's all I have to say to you. Good evening.'

'Good evening,' I replied, words I don't think I've ever used before, but I was still in shock. I added, 'Thanks for calling round.'

Edgar stopped for a second. 'Yes, I think that went quite well, really – certainly better than most of my conversations.'

Tuesday 5 November

6.30 p.m.

The day before my audition.

I've got to be word perfect. So I've been rehearsing in front of the mirror, speaking into a banana. I'm using that as a microphone. I've even been saying, 'Is this banana on? One, two, three.'

But I keep thinking about Edgar too. I

don't know what was more amazing . . . Edgar rolling up at my house, or what he said about Maddy liking me.

Even Edgar looked surprised as he said it, as I'm sure he thinks Maddy is way out of my league.

But I will definitely take a chance and ask her out. I've just got to pick the right moment.

Wednesday 6 November

8.00 a.m.
A text from Maddy:

A big day.
So dream big.

2.30 p.m.
I've only told a couple of people at school this time about my audition. But the word must have got round, because tons of people have been asking me about it – shockingly, a few even wished me 'Good luck.'

Now the people at my school still think I'm from Planet Weirdo. And I still get a few 'Yo,

where's your dad?' and 'Tell your dad laters.'
But I think they're beginning to get used to
me here now – which is a start.

And most days Julie and I have a laugh
together (and she thinks all our laughing is
really building up her immune system). Holly
makes a point of coming over and talking to
me too, while totally ignoring every other boy
in my year (and yeah, I like that. A lot).

So I shan't be changing schools again, after
all. Well, you can't keep swapping back and
forth, can you? Not sure my old school would
have me back anyway. So it looks as if my
current dump is stuck with me.

2.45 p.m.

I don't think I can write any more about this
afternoon's (*this afternoon's* – HELP!) audition. It's getting me too worked up. I just want
to get it over with now. So no more until after
I've done it.

5.15 p.m.

Well, just a bit more, because it's kind of cool
rolling up at the recording studio, which is
right next to the local radio offices. It doesn't

look much from the outside, to be honest –
boring old offices with tons of cars and vans
outside.

But inside there's a buzz right away. And
while Dad was telling the receptionist about
the VIP(!) he was accompanying, Maddy and
I watched people tearing about. One girl was
babbling away into a walkie-talkie. 'We can't
push the timing back any more. We're right
up against it now.'

Then a guy brandishing a clipboard whisked
us down a dimly lit corridor and into a room
with dark walls, which didn't look much
bigger than my bedroom. And far less cosy.

Evie was already there and she introduced
us, in a worshipful whisper, to the associate
producer of the show. He was slouched and
tired-looking and peered at me through huge
glasses. I was too nervous to catch his name.

The cameraman, Marty, was chirpy and
friendly though. He told me where to stand
and Evie told me to just relax and forget
about the cameras. Not easy, especially when
a camera suddenly came to life and shot
towards me. It swept nearer and nearer until
it was practically in my lap.

Then I was peering into this great, glassy black hole. I've seen friendlier-looking monsters on *Dr Who*. I was supposed to be funny in front of *that* – and in this dark gloomy cupboard? Maddy and Dad kept smiling reassuringly at me. But Evie and the producer were whispering together in the corridor.

What about? Was it to do with me? I hadn't a clue, but there was a definite air of tension now. In fact, this felt just like the start of an exam. You know what, I have a horrible feeling this is not going to go well. This is just too cramped and drab for comedy. Plus, that camera keeps looking at me so oddly.

No time for any more.

7.00 p.m.

It's all over.

Shortly after my last entry the red light went on and Evie whispered, 'Give it the best you've got, Louis.'

And that was it. I was off.

Desperately trying to be funny while the camera circled me, I told myself, *I can do this* – but I had one problem. I wanted to cough. I did my best to stifle it. That only made it worse though, and all at once I released the weirdest cough the world has ever heard. In fact, it brought back memories of being taken to the zoo to watch the sea lions at feeding time.

So here I was, at the most important audition of my life, impersonating a hungry sea lion. The light snapped off. The camera swirled back and I gulped down some water. Then I scrambled about for my hankie, because my eyes had started watering too.

I was falling to pieces here.

'You're not nervous, are you?' Evie asked softly, confidingly. Of course I was, but I knew the moment I admitted that, I'd definitely be marked down as an amateur. 'Quite promising,' they'd say, 'but couldn't take the pressure. What a shame.'

But I can take pressure.

That's why I said quickly, 'No, I'm never nervous. I'm just getting over a cold. I'm totally cured now, though.'

I took a deep breath, and very nearly coughed again. But then I was off. I even started to get used to that giant, glassy eye, and actually I think it went well. Dad and

222

Maddy laughed – but of course they would. Evie laughed too, though, and Marty grinned away. As for the associate producer – Mr Chuckles, as I call him – well, he looked just as fed up when I'd finished.

Evie said, 'That was excellent.' (But maybe she said that to everyone.)

'Have I won then?' I joked.

'You're the last one we've seen and you're certainly in with a chance, I can tell you that,' said Evie. 'But all eight of you will go up on our website now. We're inviting comments, but the final decision will be made by us' – she pointed at the associate producer – 'after we've watched them all again at a meeting on Friday evening. We're looking for someone who is extremely talented, of course. But also the person who would best fit into our All-Winners Final. As soon as we've decided we'll either ring or text you.'

Ring if you've won – text if you haven't, I thought.

'But it probably won't be until about half-past eight on Friday, as I think it's going to be a tough decision,' said Evie. 'You're all just so good.'

Outside, Maddy said, 'That was the best you've ever done it. You were perfect.'

And Dad said, 'I'm very hopeful.' Then he added, 'Only about forty-eight hours to wait.'

Keep everything crossed.

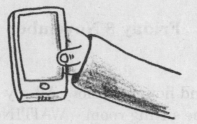

CHAPTER NINETEEN

A Message from Evie

Thursday 7 November

9.30 p.m.

Today is somewhere I just really don't want to be.

I want to fast forward this whole day and speed into tomorrow, then I'll know if ... but you don't need me to write any more, do you?

Of course, the whole day has ambled along tragically slowly, as the waiting for news goes on and on ... and, er, on.

Friday 8 November

8.25 p.m.

Any second now, I'll know. All my family are here in the sitting room – WAITING.

Elliot's just suggested that if I put my mobile close to the window it'll be in a better spot for reception so I've done that. No doubt I'll move my mobile again in another five minutes.

Maddy's looking as tense as me, and Mum keeps offering round food which no one (apart from Elliot) can eat, while Dad is just looming in the doorway, saying stuff like, 'Just remember, you've done very well to get this far, Louis.'

Twenty minutes ago my phone did ring. I leaped up to hear my grandad ask if I'd heard anything yet. We had a very brief conversation. (What if Evie was trying to get through at that very moment?) Maddy said, 'We have to hear something very soon now.'

8.45 p.m.

Finally, finally Evie has been in contact. Only my heart sank when I saw she'd sent a text.

'If it was good news she'd have called me,' I said.

'Not necessarily,' said Maddy at once. But she sounded disappointed too.

Actually it wasn't good or bad news.

Instead, she was telling me that she and Giles (so that was the associate producer's name) were having great difficulty deciding, as the standard was so very high. They were still keenly discussing who to pick and it might not be until later tonight or tomorrow before they decided on their choice.

'So you're still in with a chance,' said Mum.

'More than a chance,' said Maddy. 'I watched all the acts on YouTube' – my nerves were jangling too much for me to do that – 'and you were by far the best.'

But Maddy was a bit biased. And the thought of not knowing until tomorrow now . . . I didn't think I could stand it.

Mum took Elliot off to bed and Dad went off to finish sorting out something in the hut.

'I suppose I should go too,' said Maddy. I was so lost in my own disappointment I hardly heard her. She'd left before I'd realized it. I nearly texted her to come back, but I didn't think I'd be very good company. I was too restless and strung up to talk to anyone for very long – even Maddy.

CHAPTER TWENTY

Lots of News

Monday 11 November

5.20 p.m.

Nothing has happened for a couple of days and now so much has happened.

It all started when I was taking a cup of tea over to Dad in the hut, just for something to do really. I was also chewing a Rolo – Mum had said I must eat something as I hadn't all day because of waiting for you-know-who to call.

Dad was on the phone when I arrived. But he quickly rang off, took the tea and asked, 'Still no news?'

I shook my head.

'Well, I've got a bit of news for you – you might not think it's good news now, but it is really.'

Dad had my full attention now. He was about to tell me about losing his job, wasn't he? At last!

But instead he said, 'We've fixed up that tutor for you.'

I'd forgotten all about that and I was too horror-struck to do anything except cough up my Rolo.

After I'd recovered Dad said, 'But I think you'll be pleased when you hear who it is – it's Todd.'

Todd was the actor who'd coached me in English and maths while I was between schools. And I liked him as much as I could like anyone who called themselves a tutor.

'Todd is waiting for one or two projects to work out, so he is resting at the moment.'

'That's a shame,' I said. 'I'm sure he'd be brilliant if someone gave him a chance.'

'True, but every cloud . . . he's something of an expert on the eighteenth century.'

'I suppose someone has to be, but actually it would be handy to know a bit of what's going on in history.' I didn't realize I was going to say that. Dad looked more than a bit surprised too.

And if I had to have a tutor, Todd would be my number one choice.

'OK, all right, we'll give Todd a go,' I said. 'Poor old Todd, resting again. Still, it happens to everyone at some time, I suppose. Are you resting at the moment, Dad?'

I thought I'd asked Dad with truly mega-tact. But I couldn't wait about any longer. I had to know if he really had lost his job.

Dad straightened up and stepped back from me. He was shocked. 'You saw copies of some emails I'd received, didn't you?'

'I accidentally knocked them onto the floor, but I only glanced at them for a second anyway.'

'I wondered if you had. Well, it's just a very little set-back.'

'Sure, but Dad, you are out of work right now.'

'I've taken voluntary redundancy.'

'So, not sacked then?' I said.

Dad gave a thin smile. 'Sort of sacked – but with some money.'

'That can't be bad.' Then I added, 'I don't get it, because when Rup was here you seemed like top mates.'

'Did we?' said Dad slowly. 'Well, I tried so hard to fit in with his new regime and show him I was still full of fresh ideas. But in the end I think he just wanted new blood.'

'He sounds like a vampire.'

'It wasn't only me – all us greybeards are out.'

I was disgusted and dead shocked. Dad was brilliant at his job and had worked so hard over the years.

'Hey, Dad, I'm sorry.'

'Don't be,' said Dad firmly. 'Rup's done me a favour really. It's time for a change, and new opportunities. And I've got so many meetings set up already with friends and contacts. One looks especially promising. So it's all good.' But I knew Dad was glossing over how he really felt. He was having a rougher time than he was letting on.

'We're not telling Elliot,' he said suddenly.

'Sure, fine.'

'And will you do me a favour?' he asked.

'Just name it,' I said.

'What's happened is nothing I can't handle. I want you to concentrate . . . well, you've got your whole life ahead of you, and I want it to be full of good stuff. That's what's important. So will you just forget about this little hiccup?' Then Dad gave a small smile. 'My world – not yours.'

'Hey, that's my line,' I said. It was the very phrase I'd used in my act about parents.

But right then I understood why Dad hadn't told me before about losing his job. And it wasn't because he was too proud or ashamed. Dad kept silent because he wanted to protect me from bad stuff like this. And sorting it out was something he'd deal with all by himself. His world – not mine.

'So don't give it another thought. Deal?' asked Dad. He was looking right at me now. In his own way I thought he was quite brave. Even a bit of a hero. 'Deal, Louis?' he persisted.

I nodded, but I so wanted to say something to him too. And there was a piece of news I could tell Dad which I thought he'd really like to know.

'You know what, Dad?' I began.

'What?' he said.

'You'll laugh when I tell you.'

'Go on, then.' Dad was sort of smiling already.

'Well, the thing is, Dad. Really, you are in fact – cool.'

Dad did laugh then, and shook his head. 'Oh no, I heard your act and I know now parents can never be cool. They're either—'

'But,' I interrupted eagerly, 'there's another rule which says when parents stop trying to be cool that's when they can be truly cool.'

'You've just made that rule up, haven't you?'

'I have, actually.' I grinned. 'But it's still one hundred per cent true.'

'Well, it's good to know,' said Dad slowly, 'that somehow I've ended up being cool after all. And I'll try and not let this news go to my head.' He grinned back at me.

Dad and I were about to leave when Mum rushed into the hut, waving my mobile about. 'Louis, you've just had a text,' she said.

'A text. That's not good, is it?' I said.

'You don't know that,' said Mum. Dad murmured in agreement.

But it probably wasn't. I bet Evie was texting, *Thanks for trying but we've picked the juggler or the conjurer or the pigeon impersonator* . . . and I so didn't want to read that. Luckily, though, I have nerves of chilled steel.

So I read my text from Evie and it said . . .

I started to sway. I tottered back from my phone. 'Mum and Dad, would you just confirm one thing – this *is* what they call real life, isn't it?'

'What did the text say?' asked Mum, looking at me excitedly. Dad was right beside me too.

'Evie says . . . she and Giles have now finally decided on their choice – and *it's me*. She's going to ring me tomorrow morning to firm up the details, but she thought I'd like to know right away. And if I wake up now I'm going to be so furious.'

'Oh, well done!' said Mum.

'Thoroughly deserved,' said Dad.

'If Elliot's still awake we must tell him,'

said Mum. 'He really has been wanting you to get through.'

'And Maddy,' said Dad. 'You must send her a text right away.'

'Of course,' I began, but then I stopped. No, she deserved to hear such red-hot news in person. And I was going to do it right now. And straight after, I was going to ask her out. I've been waiting for the right moment. Well, there'll never be a better moment than this.

CHAPTER TWENTY-ONE

I'm Nearly on *Crimestoppers*

Monday 11 November

5.50 p.m.

In a rare burst of speed I ran all the way to Maddy's house. And then – well, I'd felt so confident about asking her out a few minutes ago but now I was feeling far more shaky.

Edgar had said she really liked me. But what if he had been lying? What if this was his final act of revenge? It could ruin everything with Maddy if I asked her out and she was just appalled, disgusted.

I couldn't be sure of her reaction at all. No boy with ears like mine could.

That's why I've now decided I'll just ask Maddy out very casually. Not make a big deal out of it at all. Then if she said 'No', or looked horror-struck, I'd hastily say something funny and we'd have a good old giggle about it.

No embarrassment at all.

As I reached Maddy's house the door was flung open and I heard a voice call, 'Put that in the bin, will you, Maddy?'

So Maddy was about to dart round the back of the house. How about if I hid behind one of the bins and then jumped out at her? That would start things off in a truly hilarious fashion.

I must admit it sounded a better idea then than it does now. Now it sounds totally moronic. But then I was giggling madly to myself as I crouched down beside the big black wheelie bin. This was going to be so hilarious.

I could hear Maddy's footsteps and I tried hard not to breathe. Then she thumped a bag into the bin. I leaped out from my hiding place, grinning madly. 'I am the genie of the bin.'

Maddy let out a loud scream, at exactly

the same moment I spotted someone running towards us, also carrying a bin bag. Someone who looked exactly like Maddy.

This was because it *was* Maddy. And the gasping, screaming figure was, in fact, Maddy's mum. This was terrible – I wanted the bin to open up and swallow me.

'Don't be alarmed,' I said, trying to smile reassuringly. 'It's me, Louis, we have met several times actually. And I'm so sorry but I thought you were Maddy. You look just like her in the dark – even though you are, of course, much, much older . . .' I was gabbling wildly while Maddy's mum was still gasping and spluttering. Maddy was right beside her now. 'Are you OK, Mum?'

'Oh, yes, yes,' she said. 'It's just when Louis jumped out at me . . .' She peered at me. 'How long have you been hiding there?'

'Oh, not long at all,' I said hastily, in case she thought I spent most evenings lurking behind her bins. 'I was just coming to see Maddy and I thought I'd surprise her . . . I'm a comedian,' I added, by way of explanation.

After that it all ended quite well really. Maddy and her mum even had a bit of a laugh about it. But it was nearly a *Crimestoppers* moment, and to say I was horribly embarrassed would be a massive understatement. After Maddy's mum had gone I said, 'I just came round to say that I've had a text from Evie.'

'Oh . . . ?' Maddy's voice wobbled uncertainly. Like me, that news made her fear the worst.

So I waited a second or two just to milk the suspense. 'And Evie said after acres of deliberation they've made their choice – and it's me.'

'Wow, wow, but that's so great!' shouted Maddy.

She was actually dancing with joy, so I thought here was the moment to add, ever so casually, 'You've been more than a slightly brilliant agent, Maddy, and so now I think it's time for you to get an upgrade . . . and be my girlfriend too.'

I said this last bit at a speed any express train would have envied. No wonder Maddy was gaping at me. She'd also stopped leaping about. Then she demanded, 'Edgar told you to ask me out, didn't he?'

'Well, he didn't exactly tell me . . . he just came round to my house—'

'Oh, he's such a special person,' interrupted Maddy. This wasn't exactly the response to me asking her out I'd been hoping for. 'He's so misunderstood by everyone – including you,' she added sternly.

'Edgar has got hidden depths,' I agreed. 'Unlike me. I've just got hidden shallows.'

Maddy continued, 'I am sure his poetry will get published one day – that's why I'm adding him to my agency. I'm going to help him, just as he has tried to help me. I see now he only dumped me so I could find happiness.' Then she turned on me, her nose quivering furiously. 'But you haven't got a clue, have you? You scare my mum and then ask me out right by the bins. And you don't even do that properly. You just ask if I'd like an upgrade.'

'Well, the truth is, I've never asked a girl out before. I've never wanted to, actually—'

'Until Edgar put the idea into your head,' she interrupted.

'No, Edgar didn't do that. The idea has been there for a while. I just never did anything about it . . . until now.'

Then I heard Maddy's mum calling her. 'I've really got to go,' she said, 'and thanks for telling me you've been chosen for the final. That's the greatest news ever.'

'I've still got to beat the parrot,' I said.

'You'll do it,' she said confidently. She started to walk away.

'What about the not-so-great news – me asking you out?' I asked. 'Shall I try again?'

'Yeah, why not,' said Maddy. 'And next time try and say something a bit better than would I like an upgrade.'

'I'll do my best,' I said.

Tuesday 12 November

5.00 p.m.

I've just sent Maddy a text.

Here it is:

When I see you my heart feels like a kite soaring high up in the sky. I made all that up myself, Maddy. Am I on the right lines? It's true, by the way. Edgar – eat your heart out.

(I didn't text her that last bit.)

5.20 p.m.

Her reply:

You really are on the right lines, so keep writing stuff like this – and you never know. I thanked Edgar for helping you and me get together. He texted back that he hates happy endings. But I don't. Maddy xx

6.00 p.m.

And that's it. Can you believe I'm racing right to the end of another diary? So, just space now to bow very low and thank you for being such a top audience.

I hate to leave you. But actually if I have to go – well, you know how some days you feel the sun is shining like crazy on you – that's exactly how I feel now (even though it's actually bucketing down with rain). My life is bursting with possibilities and I just feel so hopeful.

No space to even tell you a final joke.

Just remember to smile on – and on.

Louis the Laugh

LOUIS'S VOCAB TIPS FOR PARENTS

Want to make sure you never embarrass
your kids again?

Here are the 'young' words you should never
use – with the alternatives which you can say.

WE SAY	YOU SAY
INNIT	ISN'T IT
CHILLAX	CALM DOWN
WICKED	LOOKS GOOD
YO, DUDE	HELLO
MY HOMIES	MY FRIENDS
HEY FAM	GREETINGS
AWESOME	IMPRESSIVE
YO, BLOOD	HELLO MY FAMILY
GROOVING TO	LISTENING TO
SOME FAT TUNES	SOME GOOD MUSIC
THAT'S SICK	THAT'S GREAT
LATERS	SEE YOU LATER
LETS'S GET AMONGST IT	LET'S GO
LET'S DANCE	I DON'T DANCE, EVER.

Finally, parents, the phrase to avoid amongst
all others is: 'I CAN STILL GET DOWN WITH THE KIDS.'

No, you can't. And saying this just makes you sound like a try-hard wannabe.

But has Louis missed out any words which should never cross a parent's lips? If so, send them to my website:

WWW.PETEJOHNSONAUTHOR.COM

I will update this list in future editions.

With special thanks to the pupils, staff and librarians at Teddington Academy for their help with this.

I LoSt to a parrot

**Have you read these other
brilliant Pete Johnson books?**

**They think I'M a big problem.
Wrong. THEY are!**

Louis can't handle it any more. All his parents
seem to care about is how well he's doing at
school (answer: not very) and what after-school
clubs he wants to join (answer: none!). They're
not interested in his jokes (his dream is to be
a comedian) and have even nicked the
telly out of his bedroom!

Can new friend Maddy help? For Maddy tells
him her parents used to behave equally badly,
until she trained them. All parents have to
be trained – and she knows how . . .

**So you think you're just a normal kid?
So did I. There was nothing strange or
special about me . . . until the night
of my thirteenth birthday.**

That's when the bombshell hits. My parents
have been hiding a huge, terrifying, life-
changing secret from me my whole life.
They're half-vampires – and it turns out
I'm about to become one too.
What. A. Nightmare.

Suddenly everything's changing. I'm growing
fangs and getting cravings for my best friend's
blood. I even smell weird . . . life totally sucks!
But that's not all. Vampires exist too – and
there's nothing more delicious to a vampire
than half-vampire blood. Things are about
to get extremely dangerous . . .

**On my thirteenth birthday, my life
changed for ever. That's when I learned
the shocking truth: I'm a half-vampire.**

Think that sounds cool? Think again!
My secret blog is the only thing that's kept
me from going completely crazy.

To complicate things even more, there have
been some vicious attacks in the woods.
Tallulah (definitely not my girlfriend) thinks
a super-vampire is behind them — and she's
desperate to prove it, with a mysterious chain
that's supposed to glow red-hot when
a vampire is close by.

I have a horrible feeling that the chain's
going to turn red-hot any day now . . .

'Being normal is one choice you just don't have – and never will again. You're weird forever. Deal with it.'

I just want an ordinary life – but I've got no chance! My parents are convinced my special half-vampire power will arrive any day now, and I'm totally feeling the pressure.

Even worse, a seriously creepy Winter Fair is in town – and now we're under attack from a spooky figure with blood-soaked hands. Everyone's calling it the Blood Ghost, but I know the truth. It's a deadly vampire – the most evil we've ever faced.

Somehow me and vampire-crazy Tallulah have been roped into tracking it down. But without my special power, we don't stand a chance . . .